AUNEAIRE

AUNEAIRE

Mira Lowitz

Copyright © 2021 by Mira Lowitz

Illustrations copyright © 2021 by Mira Lowitz

First paperback edition November 2021

Edited by Sean Fletcher & Sarah Barker
Cover concept & book illustrations by Mira Lowitz
Cover illustration by Carlo Tano
Book design by Veronica Scott

ISBN 979-8-9851509-0-2 (paperback)

www.miralowitz.com
or
Instagram Auneaire

Content warning: this book contains imagery related
to death and dying.

Five unexpected leaders are in for a treat—

Will they complete the prophecy or meet their defeat?

Divyeine could shed blood as rain

And three leaders shall die, the rest live in pain

As useless as icebergs sit

Two shall drift—their lives will split

Eventually they'll find their way

Else the other tribes Divyeine will slay

To stop the fighting

They'll bring the moonstone to Divyeine from Kieling

The plea for help is strong and clear

But hope has risen and help is near

Ian

LARVESON

Natalia

MELIANDOR

Micah

DIVYEINE

Fiomi

KIELING

Levie

SEMBERIC

TRIBES

Divyeine - the tribe of war

Kieling - the tribe of intelligence

Larveson - the tribe of music

Meliandor - the tribe of beauty

Pembermane - the tribe of art

Talaskin - the tribe of truth

Semberic - the tribe of the dead

The seven tribes were created in Auneaire so they can build each other up, not knock each other down. Each tribe must work with one another in order to individually complete successful lives of peace, love, creativity, and balance.

PROLOGUE

I MEET HIM AT MIDNIGHT. A smooth breeze whips my hair—not too strong—not like the raging winds that nip at your skin, sending needle-sharp pricks that hurt. The breeze dusts up a few red and golden leaves. The light yellow moon glows soft and bright. It seems to be smiling down at me.

I skip to our meeting spot—the lone willow tree that stands in the middle of our society. The mark of earth. The value of real nature. The significance of pure life. The Willow.

I run my fingers over the rough bark of the Willow, catching on a few loose pricks of wood splinters. The long, green tendrils glisten, illuminated by the moon's glow.

I see him. Standing in front of me. Ian. The only friend I've ever known. I rush toward him and throw my arms around him.

"Micah," he breathes in my hair, shallow, his seven-year-young voice breaking the calmness of the night.

"Ian," I respond.

"Did anyone see you?" Ian says, worry edging into his voice.

I roll my eyes. "No," I say. "No one."

A sigh of relief slips from Ian's lips. The two of us slide down the trunk of the Willow. Ian snakes his hand into mine. I give him an innocent little kiss on the cheek.

"If anything ever happens, Micah, I just want to let you know..."

"Yes?" I ask.

"I—"

"Micah Bourrow!" I gasp and wriggle my hand out from our woven mess of fingers. "You come here this instant!" My mother's slim figure points a shaky finger at me. She stalks toward me from behind the tree, and I stumble away. I wasn't aware that she had followed me from home. Was I too loud when I left the house?

I let out a cry of panic. "Ian!"

My mother pinches my ear, twisting it in a sickening way. I yelp, grabbing blindly at what I hope to be Ian. But it's just air.

"You will never see that filth again!" my mother threatens in a dangerously low voice. Her anger takes hold of her. She upper-cuts my nose; a disturbing crack fills the quiet space. Pain crackles throughout my body, pain so severe my vision goes black as I again stumble. Blood spurts from my nose. My voice is shrill as I scream.

"Ian!" I scream, but I hear no answer. "Ian! Ian. Ian ..."

Things used to be so perfect. Everything was perfect, with Auneaire united at last, all the tribes working together. Life was perfect. But I should've known that there's no such thing as perfect. It's just a word, meaningless because life doesn't use it in its beauty. Nothing is perfect, and it would've been better had I known that before.

oNE

"ARE YOU READY?" LEONIE ASKS ME.

I pull down my tight-fitting dress. It has a gold collar, and jade green satin flows down to a knot, slipping down to a short skirt. The sides of my stomach and back are showing. Usually I would feel self-conscious, but I don't today. Where we are going will be dark enough for me to not feel self-conscious. I slap on a little makeup—some mascara, light lipstick, and a thin layer of concealer, but that's it. Divyeines don't wear makeup. If they do, it's for a special occasion. I'm wearing it to hide my hurt.

I stare at a faded photograph of two young children smiling broadly at the camera. I remember when Ian took the photo. I had skipped fencing classes to meet him at the Willow. He had come with a small blue backpack. He was wearing his usual blue sneakers, a green shirt, and jeans. Every time we met he would wear those sneakers, which was so often that they became very ripped and dirty. I was wearing stone gray cargo pants, a tank top, and a cardigan, which is my usual outfit. My hair was short then, barely shorter than my chin, and I had pulled it back from my face in a half-up, half-down hairstyle. Ian had unzipped the backpack and pulled out an old camera. We set it on a rock, sat down on the grass near the Willow, and waited for the timer we set on it to go off. The camera buzzed as the film emerged. After we waited for the film to develop, Ian gave it to me. Because of the low light, our faces were quite grainy, so it is hard to tell it was us, but this photograph is important to me. I've kept it ever since. The photo has become worn, and its edges have yellowed. Ian, I think, closing my eyes. I haven't seen him in so long.

"Micah!" Leonie says loudly. "Are you ready?"

"Huh?" I ask, frazzled by my thoughts. "Yeah, I guess." I glance at the photograph one last time before my gaze focuses on my friend.

"Okay, let's go over. I've already told your parents I'm taking you shopping."

"So late at night?"

"I've got it covered. You see, there's something new called

night shopping. Try it sometime."

I snort. "More like night shoplifting."

"Ah!" Leonie says, obviously displeased. "You're no fun. And we're not shoplifting. We're going to a party, Micah. Well, my party to be exact."

She's wearing a pink camisole that's cropped so short it's practically a bra and matching pink leggings. Her hair is plaited in a braid that she brushes over her shoulder. Her face is thick with makeup. I guess she inherited the love for makeup from her mother. Her lips are glossed with the best and reddest lip gloss she could buy. Her eyes are slicked with mascara that doesn't clump. Her cheekbones are streaked with bright, glittery smears of highlighter. She had brought her supplies to help me get ready, even though it's her party that we're going to.

Leonie and I emerge from the hallway to the living room. Father is sitting on the couch, a book about combat techniques resting on his lap. He looks up for a fleeting second, but his eyes return to his book. Mother doesn't even look at me. She slams her liquor bottle on the counter and stumbles toward the sink to cough up phlegm.

"I'm going, Mother and Father."

"Where are you going, daughter?" Father asks, looking like he couldn't care less.

"Leonie already told you, Father. We're going shopping. I just need to buy new leggings."

Mother spins around, glaring at me with sunken, bloodshot eyes. "What's wrong with the ones you have?" That's as pleasant as she can get. Leonie and I both know that even when she's not wasted, she isn't particularly the nicest, even to my friends.

"Yesterday I tripped during hand-to-hand classes because of my boot laces, and I shredded my leggings. We were practicing without the mats."

"That serves you damn right. You gon' get killed if you get tripped up 'cause of your boot laces." Her words slur together, but I know she'll be up until I get home.

I feel too tired to argue, so I just bade my parents goodbye as Leonie and I step out into the chilly air. Divyeine likes to keep the temperature of the tribe low. They want it to be more realistic for when we "go out into the real world," but honestly, I don't think we ever will. The only problems that erupt are little things that need some enforcement, just to keep everyone safe.

The street is dark. Every house we walk past seems to go by slower and slower. The neighborhoods are cookie-cutter, each house built the same way as the adjacent one. Only Divyeine has cookie-cutter neighborhoods. I've seen maps and pictures of the neighborhoods in the other tribes, but I've never actually been to them before. There is one porch light for every house; the glow from the lanterns lights the way. There are no streetlights, no cars—though cars aren't usually used around here anyway because the expanse of neighborhoods is only a few miles or so. There are just the sounds of our shoes crunching the dirt road and of our shallow breaths.

Leonie's house is probably the farthest it could possibly be. Her house is located near the Willow. Walking into her house feels like walking into my own because they are built the same.

The atmosphere of the party is loud. And bad. *If Ian were here...* I think. No. He wouldn't be here in Divyeine. He's too good to be here. In fact, I'm not even supposed to be here. Kids from Divyeine are not allowed to hang out with the other tribes. Though the other tribes can hang out with one another, two people from different tribes can't reproduce with one another. It's forbidden. Leonie didn't tell me that other tribes are here. But somehow, I just know. I have a feeling.

I'm only friends with Leonie because she is in Divyeine. She used to live in Meliandor, staying out of sight and on the down low until some Meliandor folks saw her being disruptive and aggressive to another child. That's when the Divyeine authorities were alerted. Every Meliandor child is too caught up in doing their own makeup to even acknowledge anyone around them, so it was strange that Leonie was harassing another child. So Leonie switched tribes. Leonie's father, Mr. Finne, fell in love with a woman from Meliandor, and that's how Leonie came to be. Usually, when something like this happens, the baby is killed immediately and so are the parents for betraying their own tribe. There was some sort of negotiation because Mr. Finne is part of the Divyeine government, so they made an exception. I don't know the details. All I know is that it was a one-time thing, and we're not allowed to switch tribes. Period. Divyeine soldiers only marry other soldiers. We don't mingle with the other tribes. We can't. But at this party, with other tribes, I know I can.

People are standing, holding cups that contain liquids I wouldn't want to drink. Leonie never mentioned that these people were from other tribes, but it is easy to tell them apart from one another. Meliandors wear too much makeup. Pembermanes dress in very creative clothes. Kielings always correct others on facts they have wrong. Lots of us like to gossip, but Kielings always seems to know the truth of everything. I've never personally talked to a Semberic, but just from listening to other peoples' conversations, it seems Semberics like to crack a lot of jokes about death. I guess they have to make the most out of burying all the people in Auneaire. Talaskins can't stop talking, Larvesons can't stop singing, and Divyeines, well, we're just boring as heck. All we really know is how to fight, how to stand guard. We always try to be alert.

I spot men dressed in crisp suits without any wrinkles, dark glasses covering their eyes. Escorts. For the people who didn't come from Divyeine, for the people from other tribes who had to go across the border, to go past the Willow tree, to get to a party no one is supposed to attend.

There's Leonie, with her strawberry blonde hair and light freckled skin. Even in the low light of the party, her makeup is highly visible. I know she used to be from Meliandor, but her makeup is too much. And her makeup is a mess. She never really was an incredibly talented makeup artist. She's talking with another girl, who is outrageously beautiful. It could be her makeup, but we rarely see beauty like that around here. She's definitely not from Divyeine. Soldiers don't usually care about beauty. They're all built the same way: with the instinct to fight instead of working it out another way. They very rarely think of taking care of themselves, instead heeding their parents, teachers, and everyone else above them. Also, they're too busy fighting. Personally, I've never really been into fighting. Only training. I'm not even officially a soldier. I don't want to go to war. I don't want to see the terrors soldiers face. I already have to deal with my own.

Sometimes I wonder if Leonie ever wants to go back to Meliandor. And yes, her demeanor isn't particularly the nicest, but I don't think she has the guts to enforce the law and harm citizens who are being troublesome.

Annoyed, I march up to Leonie. "What is this?" I demand. "You never said I'd be going to a party with other tribes. Why would you invite the other tribes?" Her father would never accept Leonie hosting a party like this. But he's out of the neighborhood, at a meeting with the tribe leaders.

She looks at me and speaks with salt on her tongue. "I didn't? Oh well. I'm sure you wouldn't mind if you saw someone here, a certain someone? Plus, no Divyeine boys are fun."

"What do you mean?" I say angrily. *Don't bring Ian into this*, I think. *Please don't.*

Leonie scoffs. "Seriously," she says, "I see you staring at that photograph. Who is he, anyway? Someone super important, I bet." She mocks me and clicks her tongue. Leonie is nice occasionally, and while I wish I could be hanging with someone else, I take what I can get.

I glare at her face and turn away, coloring deeply. "Ian," I say. "His name is Ian."

A boy standing in front of me turns around. "Did you say my name?"

Two

"IAN?" I SAY IN A SMALL VOICE. I recognize his eyes. Soft, but alert. Light brown. The same as I remember. But no. It can't be him. It can't. It just can't.

We went through so much together, and to think that we would reunite after eight years, like this? Thoughts run through my head. What if he doesn't like me anymore? That was probably why he left, right? Am I just overthinking things? He might hate me.

I blink. Ian is standing there. Waiting for an answer. "Did you say my name?" he asks. I snap back to present. I'm glad what I just imagined isn't real. Not yet, at least. I can't mess this up.

"Ian?" I say.

Ian brightens and emits the biggest smile I've ever seen him make. "Micah," he whispers. He steps forward quickly, and without hesitation, he wraps his arms around me and holds me tight. I feel safer than I have. Better than I have. Happier than I have. In a long, long time.

"Micah," he cries softly, a single glistening tear sliding down his cheek. I brush the pad of my thumb against his cheek to wipe his tear away.

"You don't need to cry," I say gently. "I'm here."

"Am I dreaming?" he asks, holding my head to his chest firmly. I breathe in all his smells. He smells like he used to. His faint aroma of almond and vanilla. It comes from the soap in Larveson.

I laugh-cry. "Am I?" I turn to Leonie.

"Leonie, this is Ian." Leonie's jaw drops. "The Ian I hoped to see again. How do you know Ian? You invited him here to your party, right?" I grin.

"Leonie?" Ian says. "Oh, she's just my friend."

"Girlfriend," Leonie corrects Ian grumpily. I stare at the two in shock. Since when does Ian have a girlfriend? And from another tribe?

Ian stares at her. "Can I talk to you for a second?"

It doesn't seem like Leonie has much of a choice, but she says defiantly, "Fine."

Ian and Leonie walk a few meters away. Leonie crosses her

arms and juts out her hip. "What's this about?"

"We," Ian says, pointing to Leonie and himself, "are not together. Have I made that clear?"

"But…" Leonie argues. "We kissed!"

"Look," Ian says. "It's complicated. You kissed me. I barely even knew you! You see, I think I'm in love with someone else." Oh jeez. We're still young. We have time for romantic drama later in life. *Give me a break,* I think.

"You think? Who could that be?"

Ian glances dreamily my way. "I'm in love with Micah. I've been in love with her since we were seven years old." Me. Me?! That's not right. I've known Ian for so long. That's really not right. That's wrong. Leonie glares at me and stomps away.

Why would he still love me after all these years? And after he left me, too. Why would he say that right now? I loved him, once. That feeling has faded. I don't know that much about love anyway. There were a lot of words that were never said before, and there's too much for me to take in now to say them. We were seven years old then. Not even adolescents. Yet, there's still something that connects us. The feeling of romance isn't mutual anymore, but we still have love. It's probably why I kept the photograph. Still, is that what he was going to say all those years ago, before my mother interrupted him and everything went wrong?

"We are done, Micah. DONE!" Leonie yells. Ian walks back to me.

He glances at me hopefully.

"Ian," I say. "This isn't right. Look, I love you, but I've only seen you for a short time, only, like, a few minutes, and I don't think I can take all this in at one moment. I love you, but not like ... that." I wring my hands together. I look up at him.

"I get it," he says. "Honestly, I don't really know what to say ..."

"I—" I start, but his gazed is focused on something behind me.

THREE

THE SOMETHING THAT IAN IS FOCUSED ON TURNS OUT TO BE SOMEONES. One pale girl, her face colored with freckles, stares at Ian and me in amazement. Her fiery red hair is tied up in a loose bun. Another girl smiles. Her skin is dark brown, her lips red, her eyes made of fire. Courage. But also that petty look of prettiness that doesn't come from Divyeine soldiers. The last person is a boy. I've seen him around the party. His blond hair is brushed to the side, and his blue eyes sparkle. I have to admit, he's kind of handsome. He, too, looks at me like I'm some kind of god.

"Oh my gosh!" the dark-skinned girl exclaims, fanning her face with her fingers. "Did you just reject Leonie Finne?"

"Uh—" Ian starts, but I help him.

"Yeah, he did. But let's not have a conversation about this. I'm sure Ian wouldn't want us to have a conversation about this."

"Oh, hi. Forgot to introduce myself," the dark-skinned girl says. "I'm Natalia Cate, and this," she gestures to the red-haired girl, "is Fiomi Bianco."

"Hi!" Fiomi says shyly.

"And I'm Levie, Levie Tanelo." Levie reaches out to shake my hand. My stomach flutters. Ian might be reading my mind because he turns to look at me almost angrily. Almost.

"Micah Bourrow." Huh. Levie Tanelo. There's something so familiar about him, but I can't pin it down. He gives off a very regal feeling.

"Ah!" Natalia grins. Her eyes twinkle the prettiest brown. "I know you! You're the one who met a boy at the border, right?"

Panicked, I glance at Ian for help. He seems as dumbfounded as I am. I reach up and pull him close by his collar so my lips are almost touching his ear. "Who told?" I whisper.

"I don't know," Ian responds.

"Hey." I release Ian's collar and turn back to the others. "Which tribes are you in?"

"Meliandor."

"Kieling."

"Semberic."

Of course! If Natalia is from Meliandor, then Leonie must

have told her. "Do you know Leonie as a close friend?" I ask Natalia.

Natalia shakes her head. "No, my friend invited me here," she says. Then she adds another statement like she's reading my mind. "But Leonie tells my friend everything that happens in Divyeine. And, well, you know Meliandor." It makes sense now. People from Meliandor usually gossip when they do their makeup or whatever they do there.

I find out that Natalia and Fiomi are best friends. Fiomi seems comfortable enough with Levie to give me the feeling that they know each other from somewhere, but it doesn't feel like they are friends. It's interesting to meet new people. These three are some of the first people I've ever met who didn't live in Divyeine, and they aren't like I expected. I feel a little cautious around them. We could be punished severely if Divyeine finds out this party exists. Also, there's something else that makes a slight feeling of negativity push its way through my body.

"It must be nice to be able to hang out freely with the other tribes." I smile softly. Levie excuses himself from the conversation for a moment. My eyes follow him to a blonde girl he starts walking toward. Must be a friend he knows. She curtsies. I wonder if that's something they do in Semberic. They disappear into a room. Is it weird to get a pang of jealousy even though Levie and I just met?

"Yeah," Natalia says, "It's pretty nice. I gained a lot of memories."

"But," Ian says quickly, as if to comfort me for the experiences I couldn't have, "it's not always that great. Because we can meet freely, a lot of ideas are shared, and the different tribes have conflicts."

Fiomi joins the conversation. "In this world, conflict is bound to occur. It might be different for Divyeine because one idea is shared throughout the tribe. Even though we can interact with each other, we still have our own rules, customs, and ideas. When two different tribes share their ideas, some people might find it interesting, but others fight about it. Conflict is bound to occur. What I've found is that the things that dehumanize people are the things that make them human. No one has a pure enough heart to not pay a price if the desire is great enough. It's just how our brains are wired. If we want something, we take it, and that usually causes conflicts too. It all comes down to the price and the reward. It seems like you just follow your leaders because you've never really been given the chance to cause conflict. I don't know how you guys do it, but everyone in Divyeine acts so simi-

lar. It might be because of the lack of experiences or simply growing up in a place where it's all order and no freedom."

She pauses for a moment. "Sorry," she says, "I kinda said a lot
there." We stare at her.

"Wow, that's really thoughtful and observant of you!" I say.
I'm impressed. She seems really intelligent. Nothing less than
what I expected from someone who was born in Kieling. She also
gives me something to think about.

Levie comes back a few minutes later. We tell him what we
were talking about. "Yeah, I think it's good for me to interact with
other people. Being in the tribe in charge of burying corpses is not
that pleasant all the time, so it's nice to interact with other people
once in a while."

The party ends later than I had anticipated, but still early
enough that Mother won't be suspicious. I bade Natalia and Fiomi
goodbye. They slip me torn napkins with their phone numbers on
them. Levie offers me his hand, and I take it. We shake.

"It was a great pleasure to meet you." Levie smiles gently. "I
hope I can meet you again soon." A feeling in the pit of my stomach had ignited when we first met, and I haven't felt this feeling
in a long time. The last time I felt it was with Ian, when we were
seven. It's so similar, yet different. Because the feeling that I had

with Ian was cultivated over many months of talking, and after such a small amount of time interacting, I already have this feeling with Levie. Feeling my hand in his hand gave me butterflies like the ones I had when I held Ian's hand. The feeling has resurfaced, just with someone else.

Ian and I are walking out, and he gives me bad news.

"My parents kicked me out," he says.

"Kicked you out?!" I say in disbelief. "Why?"

"Because . . ." is all he says. *Because?* I think. Because why?

"I guess you could stay with me. We have to be careful though, especially after what happened eight years ago. You don't get how mean my parents are, though. Their actions have gotten out of hand. They're using their knowledge of violence on me, and it's not okay."

"Wow, look at you." Ian whistles and pushes me playfully. "All grown up." I laugh, but not for long. I pull the sleeve of my jacket up to reveal several angry dark-colored marks. The bruises trail up and down my arm, the colors contrasting against each other. Green, blue, purple, black. My arm looks disgusting, I know. Ian and I stop walking for a moment, and I pull up my sleeve to wipe the little layer of makeup off my face. Ian stares, horrified.

"What have they done to you?" Ian gasps. He gently holds his fingers to my face, careful not to touch my black eye and rough cheek, which has thin slits of scars that snake their way up to just below my right eye. No one could see my face in the low light of the party.

"I need to tell you something," I admit. Ian nods, encouraging me to go on. "Ever since my mother caught us at the Willow, all those years ago, I've come to realize that the society isn't how it was. Auneaire is being torn apart. We are no more one united community of people who work together with things we are good at to be the best we can be. Instead, we are using our powers against other tribes. And I don't mean Meliandor or Talaskin, or even Larveson are doing this, but the war tribe, Divyeine. My Divyeine, my home. They're using what they know to conquer other tribes."

Ian looks uncomfortable. "What do you mean, conquer other tribes?"

"I have something to show you," I say. He nods.

FOUR

WE SLIP IN THROUGH AN OPEN WINDOW, the sill creaking from our weight, but not too much. Mother is most likely still awake but hopefully too drunk to hear us. It's dark, and our only guide is the small beam of moonlight shining through the glass pane, illuminating my dusty wood floor. Ian creeps through the window first, and then I follow, my feet bare and cold. I had taken off my heels to avoid making a lot of noise. I thrust them into Ian's open arms, which are spread for me, not my shoes. Then, I hop off the windowsill as quietly as I can and barrel Ian over on the floor, resting my hands on his chest and my chin on his shoulder.

"I'm trusting you. They won't find me, right?" questions Ian.

I shudder. "I hope not."

Ian stares at me. I look back at him. "Oh!" I say. "I have something to show you." I get up from the floor and walk to my desk, picking up a newspaper dated today that I meant to read earlier. "Here." I gesture, handing Ian the paper. "There's something about a prophecy on the fifth page."

Ian's eyes flicker to the prophecy, his brows furrowing as he traces the words with his gaze. "What do you think it means?" I say once Ian is done reading. He hands the newspaper back to me.

"You're definitely right about one thing—Divyeine is planning to kill off the other tribes."

"But how do you know this is true? That this prophecy isn't really just some stupid hoax? How do you know that this could happen?"

"I ..." Ian trails off. "I just have this feeling that it's right. That we need to follow whatever these clues are. You need to trust me on this."

"But what about the five leaders? Who do you suppose those could be?" Us, I think.

"Us," Ian says. "It could be us."

"But what about the other three?"

"The trio we met at the party. Natalia, Fiomi, and Levie."

"Yeah," I say, dwelling on the idea. "But that doesn't make sense. We barely know each other, plus the fact that it's so random. How are we supposed to complete something if we don't really know each other?"

"You know me. And I'm here with you. Right?"

"Right," I say, looking down. I'm unconvinced, but I hope I don't sound like that. Ian grasps my hands, and I look up. "What?"

"Whatever this is, I feel it. I also feel that we are going to be two of the leaders, and the trio we met will be the other three. And that we are going to be fine. We'll be fine."

"But—" I start.

"Shh," Ian says. "No buts."

"Hey!" I glower. "How do you know that it's us? That we are the chosen leaders?"

"I know. I just know."

"Okay, fine. Say it was us. And say this prophecy is true. How can someone know the future? And what does it mean by 'Divyeine could shed blood as rain, and three leaders shall die, the rest live in pain'?" I recite part of the prophecy.

Ian doesn't answer for a moment, as if he is lost in thought. Suddenly, he turns to me and says slowly, "I think you know what it means."

Divyeine could shed blood as rain, as we are entirely capable of doing. Except that shedding that much blood would mean killing thousands of people. Who would they kill? As far as I know,

there's only one place where Divyeine could kill that many people. Auneaire. The society they protect. But why?

I make a nervous whimper, the raspy sound building in my
throat, scratching the raw flesh of my neck. I try to forget that
Divyeine might attack the other tribes by talking to Ian. "You
know," I say. "Things a few years ago used to be so perfect." I sigh,
turn my head so it's pointed to the ground, and scrunch up my
face, my lips moving to make a sad smile. "It was good back then."

"But there's no such thing as perfect," Ian points out.

"Ah! Don't ruin the moment for me," I say in exasperation. My
limbs are starting to shake, and I'm anxious even though I try not
to be.

"Okay," Ian snorts. "I think it's time I retire."

"Right, let me get you a pillow and blanket."

"Where should I sleep?"

I point to the floor. "Sorry!"

It's going to be uncomfortable sleeping on that floor. But
there isn't any room on the bed, and there is really nothing else.
My room is plain, covered only with a small, metal-framed bed
with a mattress as hard as rock. The only other thing I have is my
desk, which is smaller than average and simple. My few possessions—clothes and souvenirs—are tucked away in a small cabi-

net built into the desk. I have to stand while writing my papers. I don't have much. It's not that I'm not allowed to keep my possessions; I just don't have any really because I'm always on the move. When soldiers are at war, I'm sure they don't think about this kind of stuff. All they are trying to achieve is avoiding getting killed.

I have few items: some bottles of makeup I got from Leonie from when she was in Meliandor and the picture of Ian and me. I'm surprised my parents didn't throw that out. "Hey," I say to Ian. "Go in my closet for a sec. I'm going outside to pretend like I just got home." Ian obliges and hops into the closet, closing the door quietly behind him.

I put on my heels again, slip out the window, and go around the house to knock on the front door. Mother keeps the door locked, so I always have to knock when I come back from my classes.

Mother answers the door. "I'm back!" I say.

"Okay," she drawls. "Come in." She sits on the couch and leans on the fluffed-up pillows. "How was it?" she says lazily.

"It was fine," I say.

Mother flicks her eyes to me and to my hands. "Where are your leggings?"

Shoot. I totally forgot about the leggings. I feel my ears burn as I make up a quick lie. "I decided not to buy leggings. I'm teaching myself a lesson. I just accompanied Leonie so she could go shopping for combat boots."

"I don't care what the hell that girl Leonie shopped for. You're not punishing yourself if you don't have leggings."

"Well, I don't have a second pair. So I'm going to learn to tie my laces real well and also to be responsible."

"Don't argue with me, young lady. Devon!" she shouts into the dining room, to my father, who is pigging out on dinner.

"What?" he slurs through a mouthful of spaghetti.

"Micah is talking back to me!" She waves her hand drunkenly toward me.

Father finishes his mouthful of food and says, "Can't you deal with it yourself?"

Mother rolls up her sleeve, and she has a bounce in her gate I hadn't seen before. She clenches her fists and says, "Fine. I'll deal with it."

I'm not fast enough. She shoots her hands out and grabs for my hair. She does this before I can move aside. She holds my hair tightly while I whimper. Mother pins me to the wall, and her knuckles connect with my jaw. Blood spills out of my mouth. The familiar metallic taste warms my tongue. I can't see the blood, but

I've become all too familiar with the color to know that it's probably staining my teeth and chin red. Red, red, red. I hate this color. I hate my life.

"Stop!" I sputter while she rakes her fingers across my face. "Enough!" My anger is high, and my blood is boiling. "I ... said ... ENOUGH!"

With one agonizing rip, I wrench myself away from my mother and her hungry lust for inflicted pain. I push Mother away. The impact of my hands on her chest is hard, and she gasps from it. "What is wrong with you?!" I cry. "Don't you understand that this hurts me? And you're doing this to your own child?" I've caught her off guard. She shares a glance with my father, who waves his hand dismissively. That's the lazy man he is. It's my mother who imparts more permanent damage. She blinks at me, her breath reeking of alcohol, her eyes dilated, her face pale, her calloused fingers shaking.

"What did you just say to me?" She curses at me, making an obscene gesture. I don't care. I've already learned to push down my discomfort with people cursing.

"Yeah, you heard me, Mother." I spit out these words sourly and storm out the door. My parents caused me too much pain. The Divyeine government turned them into this. Into these monsters. All because they were forced to serve in the army. I thank their service, but war is a hellish reality, and war creates monsters.

FIVE

IT'S VERY LATE AT NIGHT NOW. I don't know where to go. So I head back to my room through the open window and shove open the closet door. Ian steps out. "That argument was horrible! Are you okay?" he asks, worry etched into his facial features.

I grumble. "I guess. It feels good to know that I finally stood up to my mother. But now I'm just frustrated because she was beating me up, and I stood up to her. I can't stay here anymore, so I'm leaving." Ian looks at me dumbfounded.

"You're what?!"

"I'm not staying here anymore."

Ian runs a hand through his hair. "So where will we go?"

"I don't know. I just can't stay here anymore. I can't stand any more of this abuse. Also, it's not like we can just head to Larveson and stay at your house." That shuts him up. We pack the few items

I have in a bag. I go to the bathroom and spit out the blood from my mouth. I stuff my toiletries in my bag, and we slip out the window again to walk in the chilly night air. I'm still wearing my short dress because I wanted to leave as quickly as possible, so my legs are cold. Ian breaks the silence and speaks.

"What now?"

I disregard his words and shiver. Silently, he wraps his wool jacket around my shoulders. I yank it off. "No" is all I say.

Ian's quiet now, unlike his usual loud, annoying, brotherly demeanor. But what do I know? I haven't seen him in years. I'm still holding his jacket, and I feel bad, so I slip my arms into it and shrug it on.

"I'm sorry," I mumble.

Ian shrugs. "Okay."

"I really am."

He looks at me. He stops walking. This doesn't feel good. "Really?" he asks. I know he's not expecting an answer. "You leave me for eight years, and you suddenly pop into my life, just like that, without a warning, and you dump all this crap on me like I'm some sort of trash can. You know, I'm really fed up with you and your ignorance, as well as your spoiled behavior. You think you can just run me over with your words, but I won't fall. I won't."

I step back in shock. Big shock. Ian threw me a curveball.

"I don't understand," I protest, but I know there's no point in arguing. I ignore that fact and rapidly start throwing things out.

"Excuse me, but I'm wondering if you thought I intended to leave you, because if you thought that, you were wrong. You were so wrong. I don't know if you remember, but my mother broke my nose that night. I was calling for you for so long. I was reaching out, but you weren't there. You think I wanted to leave? Ha! You're really, really stupid if you thought that. I didn't expect to see you at that party. I really didn't. You weren't like that. I would have looked for you every day if I could, but what good would it have done? You left me, and you didn't leave any trace of where you could be. No line of information. If you were in Larveson, I'm honestly not sure where you were living. You said your parents kicked you out. Tell me why you left me that night!"

"I left you because I was seven years old, Micah! I had big dreams, and big ideas, and I had the great plan that I would save you from your awful parents! But I never knew how terrible they truly were. I ran, Micah. I was a coward! I didn't know how bad your situation truly was until I saw it in front of my eyes. My whole plan was to save you! Save you from living such a horrible life! But I didn't do it. Instead, I ran. Not one day went by where I didn't think of you. But yet again, I was a coward. I didn't know how to reach out again. I know things are different now, but I'm back. Shouldn't that be enough?!" Ian is very silent. His face is red. He's panting, and even though he isn't speaking, a wave of emotion seeps toward me. This is what I feared. I can't let our friendship slip away. We've known each other for too long to end it.

I start to speak. "I—" He stops me there, putting a hand up.

"Stop," he says quietly, his voice cracking. My heart breaks, and I long to touch him, to hold him, to let him know that I'm sorry and that it will be okay. Even then, would my touch still comfort him, or would it make it worse? The truth of the matter is, everything I needed to say has come spilling out, and memories and old feelings have resurfaced. I had always dreamed that reuniting with Ian would be magical. That all the pain would just go away. But it doesn't. In fact, it has become even worse because the scars of those memories are opening up and becoming raw, and the pain from the lack of comfort after he left is too much to bear. "Stop, I don't need any more of your ranting on about my mistakes. I don't want to hear it." Ian is close to tears now. I can hear it in his tone and in how his voice breaks.

We stand there for a while. I hold in tears. I'm angry, and he's angry too. We're both hurt. This isn't how I wanted things to go.

"I'm sorry," I say eventually. "I didn't mean it like that. Everything is just happening so fast, and I needed to let it out."

He merely nods.

The street is dark—I don't even know where we are headed. I try to clasp my hand in his, but he shakes out his hand.

We both already stopped walking, and I put my fingers on the collar of his jacket. I go on my tiptoes and reach up to brush my lips against his rough cheek. He looks at me, but now he doesn't seem angry. All that's left is sadness, the cracks of invisible scars shining through it. He leans in closer to me so our faces are only a few inches apart. I can feel his warm breath on my lips. He looks me straight in the eyes, and I notice that his eyes aren't light brown. They're hazel, and emerald and flecked with copper and gold. I just wasn't paying enough attention before to notice. He moves closer, and closer, and I turn my head to the side.

"We better get going. I don't know where we will be sleeping for the night, and obviously we can't pass the borders to any of the other tribes without someone from that tribe spotting us."

Ian doesn't say anything. But he straightens and slips his hand into mine, still not saying a word.

SIX

WITH NOTHING TO DO, we sit on the curb of the sidewalk, a dark playground laid out behind us. The playground has no children. Of course, whoever would let their kids play in the middle of the night, well they're crazy. I wouldn't do that. Yet I'm still here, at this playground. This playground is only meant for the use of children six and under, so I'm not sure why we stopped here to rest. Everything is still, and the night is silent. It's eerily quiet when you're near a playground. Yes, it is the dead of night, but usually the playground is noisy, and I'm sure it gives more than one person a headache.

"How'd you meet Leonie?" I ask curiously. I already mentioned to him that I never thought he would be at that party, but since he was, I'm interested.

"I met her a few years back. We were both going through our

own problems, and we helped each other." He says it cautiously, like he's trying not to light a fuse that will make me explode into jealousy and rage.

"Chill, Ian," I say. "You don't have to be cautious around me. I know Divyeine is the only tribe who doesn't let their people see other tribes. I don't really care now that you're here. Plus, I don't care what you and Leonie did before she came here. I haven't known her for long." I can see Ian flash a small smile, one that's barely noticeable, but still there.

Doing nothing, my mind wanders back to Ian. And how I'm grateful I met him. There's a reason I'm not brainless like my Divyeine peers. It's because I was exposed. I'm not brainless because I met Ian. And I met Ian just in time too, before I trained too much with my Divyeine peers to become a robot without a heart, a killing machine. I was exposed to him.

I glance at Ian and say, "We should call one of the trio."

Ian shoots back, "And if they don't pick up?"

I sigh and roll my eyes. "Then call another one!"

Ian looks down. He fumbles to weave his fingers together. "Right." That word comes softly and slowly, like a baby chick who is not quite ready to come poking out of its shell.

So I take out my phone from my backpack and dial Natalia's

number from the scrap of napkin she gave me.

A shrill voice pops up from the other end of the line. "Hello?"

"Natalia!" I exclaim as I put the phone to my ear.

"Urm, I'm sorry, but who is this?"

I chuckle, Ian cocks his head to the side. "Oh, sorry. Hi, it's Micah."

"From the party?"

"Do you know anyone else named Micah?" I don't mean to sound rude, but sometimes things burst out of my mouth before I can properly think.

Natalia doesn't seem angry. Instead, she just laughs. "Haha, no, I don't."

"I have to ask you an enormous favor."

The line goes quiet on the other end. "... Yes?"

"We need to stay at your house."

"We?"

"Yes, Ian and me."

"Oh." The line crackles.

"Ah! I'm losing connection."

"Okay, fine." She tells me her address.

I nod. "Thanks," I say. "We have something to show you."

SEVEN

THE WARM GLOW OF THE LIGHT ON THE CEILING OF NATALIA'S BEDROOM BEATS DOWN ON OUR BACKS, which are hunched over in attempts to glimpse the slip of paper lying thin on the floor. Natalia's face is shadowed with confusion.

"What does this even mean?" she asks. We explain it to her as clearly as we can, taking the next half hour to talk about the prophecy and how we are in it. I do most of the talking.

Ian only says, very quietly: "It's just destiny. You have to trust destiny." Destiny may not seem like a lot to someone else, but it means a lot to us. Both of us trust destiny and believe in destiny and fate a lot. It's how we met. What were the odds that two children around the same age would bump into each other at the Willow at such an odd hour? It didn't feel like a coincidence. It was my first time doing something rebellious. I was always curious about what was outside Divyeine. I had passed by the opening to the Willow many times going to different training classes. At six years old, I left my home at midnight, and I never expected I would find someone there. But there was someone, a boy. He was wearing blue sneakers and reading a book. A lantern was lit next to him. It was my first time meeting someone outside of Divyeine. To me, it was a glorious sight. The way the warm glow of the lantern lit his young, smooth face. The way it illuminated the leaves of the Willow. After that, we started talking, and it was just a few months past my seventh birthday when my mother caught us. The first time I met Ian was the first time I started believing in fate. We still believe in fate now, and it's why we believe so strongly that we could be the leaders. The prophecy is tied to fate, so believing in fate means we could be tied to the prophecy as well.

"And what if I don't believe in destiny?" Natalia says.

"You have to," Ian says very solemnly. His silence is making me uncomfortable. I squeeze his hand for reassurance and for support. His calloused hand is hot and sticky. I want to take my hand back and wipe it on my dress. But that would be rude. So I don't. Though now, after a minute, I don't think about his sticky hand, I only think about the fact that he didn't squeeze back. It seemed almost as though his hand was limp.

Suddenly frightened, I look up in his lively eyes—or I try to—but his eyes aren't there. At least, not the eyes I know. The eyes that have taken place of the old ones are dull and broken. Ignoring Natalia's questions about the prophecy, I turn to Ian.

"Are you all right?" I ask. He doesn't answer. His eyes are blank and glossy, his face expressionless. I ask for him again and again, but still no answer. Natalia even ceases asking her questions and starts helping. My stomach knots, so I just listen. Ian's breathing is ragged and tired, and his heart is beating loud, pounding, punching at his chest, which rises and falls. I'm getting frustrated. He's not responding to us, and we can't get him to focus.

In the months that I knew him, this had never happened before. I'm starting to panic. It must have been something he developed during the years we stopped talking. I don't know what to do to help him.

"I could call Levie and Fiomi," Natalia suggests. "Maybe all four of us will bring him back to be himself."

"It wouldn't hurt," I say thoughtfully.

"Okay," we decide. "Let's call them."

EIGHT

"So ... WHAT HAPPENED?" Fiomi asks, unfolding her brown-and-black glasses. She slips them on and peers at Ian's emotionless face. Levie stands in the corner of the room. Natalia went to get them at the border, the Willow tree, because people aren't allowed in other tribes without an escort who lives there.

"Well, we were reviewing the prophecy, telling the story to Natalia—"

Questions arise.

"What prophecy?"

"Uh—"

"What story?"

Natalia squeaks. "Ugh, never mind that now. I still don't even understand it myself." She folds her fingers and glances at her nails, which are painted with a slick coat of bright pink polish.

I shake my head like I'm trying to snap out of something. "Okay. I told you the first part. Then I was holding his hand." Ignoring the surprised looks on the trio's faces, I quickly add, "For reassurance or something. We were a little bit on edge with nowhere to go."

"Mm-hmm," Fiomi mumbles. She strengthens her voice. "And what happened before? What do you mean, 'with nowhere to go?'"

"Well, you see, because I live in Divyeine, my parents happen to be aggressive, and they kicked me out because I spoke up for myself. We couldn't head to Larveson because Ian's parents kicked him out as well. I still don't know why."

I'm about to mention our fight when Ian starts shaking.

"Ian! Ian, look at me. Ian! What's going on, Fiomi? What's going on?" I say, my voice shaking with fear and panic. Ian seems to be choking on his own saliva.

Fiomi shares my look, surprised and frightened. She doesn't answer, and Ian doesn't look at me. I shake him and place my hands on his chest, leaning forward, crawling up to him, putting my weight on his chest. CPR. I have to try. I push on his chest, hard and fast. I pinch his nose and seal my lips to his and blow. Two blows, and out. His chest isn't rising. He's really choking. So

I continue the compressions, blowing and blowing. Then I stop when his chest isn't rising with the air I'm giving him. I look down at him, and without thinking, I lean down to press my trembling lips against his cheek in case I only have one last moment with him before his light burns out, but my lips have a mind of their own. They move to his lips, and they stay there. The light returns to his eyes. His chest rises and falls raggedly, and he sucks in gasps of oxygen. Levie steps away, and Fiomi and Natalia look at each other. I can't read their expressions. I withdraw from the kiss, Ian and I sharing a look of surprise.

"I—I'm sorry," I stammer, while Ian stares at me. I can't tell what he's feeling. "I shouldn't have done that. I wasn't thinking and—"

Ian kisses me back. I break away.

"I'm sorry," I say again. "I already told you. I shouldn't have done that." I don't look at him. Instead, I look at Levie. I know that when I kissed Ian, Levie sure wasn't happy with that. I don't know what's right or what's wrong now. I can feel the line of Ian's stare burning into my back. Levie's sweet, though I barely know him. And honestly, I barely know Ian either.

NINE

"WHAT HAPPENED?" Ian says meekly. He's weak, so I force him down on the carpet.

"You just started choking, I guess. I don't know why. We called Fiomi and Levie because you wouldn't respond to us."

"Right," Ian says. "That was on me. I didn't want to talk to you. As for the choking, I was diagnosed with dysphagia a few years ago. I got a head injury from a little fight I had with one of my classmates during recess."

The rest of us exchange glances but say nothing. I break the silence. "Lie down," I instruct.

"Why?" Ian complains. He's acting like a little child.

"So you don't feel dizzy," I snap. I glower at Ian, and he just smiles with a silly glance.

"I'm not dizzy," Ian's words blend together, and I know it's not from his heavy Larveson accent, where his words usually slur with twisted syllables and airy consonants. "I'm only dizzy for you." He giggles, and Levie shakes his head.

"Oh, stop it! I thought you were going to die, okay?" I sit so my back is facing Ian, to just get away from him for a little quiet. But he just drags himself to clumsily flop down next to me.

Immediately, I avoid all contact with Ian and exclaim, "I'm going to take a walk."

I stand up abruptly, and Levie follows. "What are you doing?" I question Levie.

"I'm coming too," he says.

"Oh."

"Yeah."

The awkwardness stretches from the doorway of Natalia's bedroom to the quiet hall that reaches the back door. I remember to keep my voice down in case Natalia's parents might hear. Honestly, I don't really mind if they catch us roaming around their property. Not to be rude, but Meliandor folks are pretty harmless. I'm sure the only thing they would hurt are flies or mosquitoes. I step out the back door, with Levie at my heels, and scan the area. Green grass littered with sparkling dew that had just come out of a light shower from the sprinklers.

"Wow," I breathe. "They have grass." It's so lovely to see grass. I don't get to see it a lot. The Cate family also owns a swinging chair. I have never been on one before, so I gently place myself on one side of the chair. Levie sits next to me and tightens his fingers around the edge of the seat. We rock back and forth, inhaling the fresh night scent. Well, it's not really night now. It's maybe two, or three, I can't be sure. The stars sparkle like diamonds, and the moon rays fall on us like running water. Smooth, and bright. I realize I want to get to know Levie more.

"So," I say. "How's Semberic? Are there dead people everywhere?" I clap my hand over my mouth, realizing how far across the boundary I overstepped. "Sorry!"

Levie takes it lightly. "It's okay," he says, chuckling. "No, there aren't dead people everywhere, but we are the tribe who buries all the dead people. All the corpses are sent to us. It gets disgusting sometimes, but at least I don't have to deal with them. I wish I could be in another tribe, like Leonie."

"How do you know Leonie anyway?"

"I used to meet her at the Willow."

My jaw drops. Familiarity and pain with this situation flood my brain with memories I both want to and don't want to forget.

"No way," I say blankly, my voice sounding robotic and dull. I want to be happy, but is it possible if right now I can't?

"No way what?" Levie asks me.

I sigh. "I met Ian at the Willow when I was seven. We were so close. I don't even remember how we met, but we met there anyway. And my mother found us. And she broke my nose. And she cursed at Ian, and he never came back."

"I'm so sorry!" Levie says with sympathy. "You know, Divyeine isn't the only tribe with disappointing parents. I'm doing really well in school, so my parents took that as an opportunity. I can't mess up. My parents are sweet, and I love them, but sometimes they push me too hard."

"Um, I didn't know that. But I suppose I never really thought about it."

"You probably aren't on good terms with them, huh?"

"We currently aren't speaking," I say flatly.

"Okay! That's normal. I'm okay with my parents for now. I mean, sometimes they are really good parents, and they say they are doing it so I can be better. It will mold me into something greater than I am. Something maybe greater than what I'm capable of."

"Wow." I glance at Levie. "Nice speech."

He laughs sharply. I think I'm pushing his buttons. "I'm serious!"

"All right," I comment slowly. "Am I getting on your nerves?"

Again, Levie laughs. "No," he says. "It's good you're asking questions."

"Okay," I say. "Okay."

TEN

WE CROWD AROUND THE SMALL SLIP OF PAPER ON WHICH THE PROPHECY IS WRITTEN. Levie and I have just gotten back from our forty-seven minute speeches to each other. We talked about many relatable things such as our disappointing parents and our meetups at the Willow.

"Can we just write it down on another piece of paper so all of us can see?" Ian grumbles. "The only thing in my eyesight is Micah's big butt!"

"Hey!" I argue. "My butt is beautiful. Of course, you wouldn't know that because your butt is as flat as a pancake!"

Natalia cackles. She falls over, clutching her stomach and convulsing in peals of laughter. "Oh my gosh!" She guffaws. "She got you good! She got you so good!"

Fiomi and Levie look at each other, their cheeks puffed out.

"Pfft!" Levie is unable to hold in his laughter, and he too laughs uncontrollably.

"I honestly have no clue how this is so funny," I say seriously, but my lips quirk up anyway.

"Yeah, yeah, we get it," Ian growls. His cheeks color deeply. Ian folds his arms and glares at the wall.

"Ian's correct," Fiomi mentions shyly. Her voice is quiet, as it usually is. Sometimes I wish she would speak up because, from what she has shown me before, she is intelligent, and I want to hear what she has to say.

"About time!" Natalia screeches, and she and Levie erupt in their laughter once more.

"Guys." I speak with force, struggling to keep my cool. "Calm down. We really need to look at the prophecy."

"Okay . . ." Natalia and Levie face each other with mock sadness written across their faces.

"This is important!" Fiomi yells. Or what I think is her yell. It's not really a yell. It's like someone speaking in a loud tone. "Quiet down! Let Micah talk!"

"We," I say, "are the five leaders who are going on the quest."

"How do you know that?" Levie says, doubtful.

"Destiny," Natalia and Ian muse in unison.

"Why would we believe this? Who would print this in a paper?" Fiomi wonders aloud.

"Well," I say thoughtfully, "When you were in school, did you guys ever learn that a long time ago, when Auneaire was just being developed, the original seven who created the tribes received an anonymous letter? And it was a prophecy, and of course the seven just thought it was silly, that it was just fake. But one of the seven, the one who represented Kieling, figured out the prophecy. Then whatever the prophecy was, it actually happened, and they learned their lesson. Should we really be risking it? I mean, I didn't know that Divyeine was going to do this. I would never support this." A lot of people would overlook the prophecy. They'd probably laugh and think it's a joke. I don't, and I wouldn't want to risk it.

"How are we supposed to stop an incoming execution of all the tribes? It says that we have to find our way. What the heck is that supposed to mean?" Levie says.

Fiomi stretches her supple, pale fingers to reach for the paper. "Let me see that!" Her eyes move across the page at a steady pace. "I'm confused as well. All we have to do is bring a moonstone to Divyeine and that stops a war?"

No one mentions that only two of us will do that.

"Should we tell someone? Like, should we make it public?"

Natalia says, reaching for a nail file.

"No," I say quickly. "No, if this is in the Divyeine newspaper, it'll stay there. The only person who I could think of to let this slip is Leonie, but she's brainless like the rest of them. What do you think, Ian?"

Ian gulps hard. "No."

"Oh, come on." I roll my eyes. "You were able to solve the first part of this riddle. You're a good solver."

"I don't know," Ian says reluctantly. "Why don't you try to figure it out? I'm sure it would be a good challenge for your brain."

"You should do it! You're the one who figured out the first part."

"Why are we fighting about this?" Ian yawns as fatigue clouds his face.

"Why can't you just do it?" I press.

"It would be good for your brain if you thought about it!" Ian protests.

I groan. "What is up with you stupid Larvesonians?"

The room falls quiet. No one speaks. They can only stare. Not good for me. Ian's face falls, and he looks up at me with a fleeting gaze, his eyes saying words of disbelief that never come out of his mouth.

***

There's a myth that Larveson saved the world. Somehow. Or, they tried. Then someone brought them down. Larveson tried saving the world. Not Divyeine. They brought Larveson down with words. I'm not sure how it worked. The myth was vague. They brought Larveson down with words and Larveson never fully built itself up again. It's a dull, short myth, but for us, it's grown to be superstition. Say something bad about Larveson, and Larveson goes down. I said something, and now I know that something will happen to Ian. I just don't know what yet.

ELEVEN

MINUTES TICK BY, my face growing redder and redder by the minute, and my stomach is tied in a knot.

"I'm so sorry," I say, clapping a hand over my mouth. "I wasn't
thinking, and that was insensitive of me."

After that, I say nothing. I don't move. I'm frozen in place, the
memory jabbing its way back into my mind no matter how hard I
try to push it away. It possesses my hands, my head, my eyes. A
migraine is starting to brew, but I clench my teeth, staring hard at
the ground. I can't take the silence anymore, and Levie must have
noticed.

"Hey, man," Levie says to Ian, "just do what the woman
wants."

"I don't want to do what the woman wants!" Not after that. I
can hear his thoughts in my mind.

Natalia scoffs. "Just call us girls, okay? We're flattered, but we're not women. Not yet, at least."

"So then what should I call you, fine ladies?" Ian asks with innocence, like he forgot about what happened. He's pretending. Thoughts percolate in my mind, cutting off any connections to the real world. I press my fingers against my temples, squeeze my eyes shut, and purse my lips.

We have to find our way. We have to find our way or else the other tribes Divyeine will slay. Divyeine is going to kill the tribes. I'm going to kill the tribes. I'm going to kill the tribes. I'm going to kill Natalia, Fiomi, and Levie. They're all going to be gone. I have to get them out. I have to get out. I have to go, but I can't go.

My eyes flash open and the room starts spinning. I'm going to kill everyone. Who am I? What am I? These thoughts scratch at me, but I pay no attention to them because my focus is directly pointed at a memory. Mother. When she told me to be who I really was.

"That's right," she had said, "take in that anger. Take in that pain. You know you're going to destroy the world. You know. Let yourself be angry. Let it out. You can't stop it, Micah."

"Don't say my name," I had growled. I sprang up on my feet, fists clenched. My mother jumped forward and attempted to close her fingers around my throat. I barely dodged, and her claw-like fingers trailed straight through the layer of skin under my eye as she attempted to screw up my face even more. That's how I got my scar. Blood had blossomed from the cut, and the pain left me weary.

"Why are you doing this?" I had cried.

"I'm doing this for you," she said. "I'm doing this so you can become strong." And in that moment, I knew. In that moment, she wasn't wasted. She wasn't drunk. Her mind was clear, her thoughts collected. My mother, with a clear conscience, was purposely in-flicting pain on her own daughter. After that, I had slumped down into an exhausted state, my mother running to her room, her foot-steps eventually receding into nothing. Silence. And that's exact-ly how I felt, and how I feel now. Nothing.

TWELVE

THE FIRST THING I HEAR ARE THE CRIES. The first thing I see is the carpet. The first thing I feel are soft fingers squeezing my arms, padded from Ian's jacket. The first thing I smell is a familiar odor. And the first thing I taste is blood. The metallic taste and smell of blood is something I know well. I'm unfamiliar with the wailing, but I realize that it's coming from me. The fingers aren't mine. Or my mother's. They are soft, but calloused as well. Not a girl's fingers. Ian's fingers.

"Micah," he tries over my high-pitched cries.

I gulp hard, moving my fingers to cover my ears. Tears drip down my nose, to my lips, and I taste the salt. I tremble, shaking, thinking. She was here. She was here. She knows where I am.

"She was here," I gasp, dread filling my empty stomach. I realize I haven't eaten since this morning, and I had skipped dinner to go to the party. I was so caught up in all that happened, I didn't have time to pay attention to myself.

"Who was here?" Levie asks. "There was no one here, Micah."

"She was standing in the doorway. She slit my forehead." Instinctively, I reach to touch my forehead and draw my fingers away red with blood.

"Your arm got stuck on a loose nail from the bedpost when you fainted." I can feel the line of blood sliding down my forehead.

"She was here! I promise you!"

"I think you need to calm down," Levie says gently. "You're in shock."

"If she knows where I am, she's already out to get me. She was here. I felt her touch. I could feel her hatred." I gulp, tears blinding me.

"You need to go to sleep. You're exhausted. It's 4 a.m. right now. Go to bed. But first, let me help you clean yourself," Ian says, rubbing my arms.

"I think I'll help her," Fiomi says. "I think it's best, female to female." Ian agrees.

We limp to the bathroom and switch the light on. Bright light floods my eyes, and we step on the cool tile of the bathroom floor. The bathroom is clean, spotless, and sterile, like a hospital bathroom. I stare in the mirror at my haggard, gaunt appearance, with my bruised and bloody arms and face.

Fiomi splashes cool water on my body, scrubbing softly at my arms and being careful with my face. I try not to wince.

"I'm sorry!" I wave it away.

Fiomi dries my skin and helps me into a purple nightgown Natalia lent to me.

We walk out from the bathroom, and Natalia gazes at us. "Go sleep on my bed," she says lightly. "I'll take the floor. It's fine. As for the three of you, figure out who takes the pull-out couch. The bed is big enough to share, so maybe Fiomi can share with you, Micah?"

"Yeah," I say tiredly, "Okay. That's fine. Thank you." I don't think before I crawl into the cushiony bed, pulling up the covers meekly for some protection, to feel safe. I sink into the pillow and drown in a deep, deep sleep.

THIRTEEN

I WAKE UP EARLY. My early is around 9 a.m., and I know five hours of sleep isn't enough at all, but I'm restless. I slide out of the bed, glancing at Fiomi, who is snoring softly, her arm tucked under her head. Ian is out on the couch, eagle-sprawled, his face squashed on the pillow. Levie and Natalia took the floor, and their tired bodies are curled under a mountain of blankets.

I slink to the bathroom, lock the door, and rub my eyes. I sit on the toilet, just thinking, and look in the mirror. My scabs are going away slowly, but after cleaning myself up, I can see the improvement of my bruises. My face is healing quickly, and before I know it, all that will be left are light pink scars that mark my dry skin like thin tattoos.

The doorknob creaks—someone is awake. I unlock the door and peek out, coming face to face with Levie.

"Sorry!" he exclaims sheepishly. "Were you using the restroom? Let me wait."

"No, no!" I exclaim. "I'm done." I usher him in, closing the door
in his face abruptly, but not before I suppress a small smile.

Everyone else is still sleeping. They are out cold with fatigue
and exhaustion, so I don't really know when they are planning on
waking up. Fiomi has taken up the whole bed, lying in a star shape.
I tiptoe over to Ian, who is now in a fetal position, his hand hanging off the edge of the pull-out.

"Hey," I say, shaking him. I'm not shaking him roughly, for I'm
still weak and tired. There's enough room, so I curl next to him,
my back to his, facing the bathroom door. I close my eyes, breathing in his sweet scent, letting my muscles relax. I slip in and out
of consciousness during the next hour, waking up to glimpses of
Levie looking at me and Fiomi and Natalia chuckling quietly, si-
dling up to each other and cozying in each other's arms. They're
good best friends.

Eventually, I sit up, yawn, and lock myself in the bathroom
again, changing into an extra pair of clothes I brought in my backpack. Baggy pants printed with the usual army green camouflage
stretch down my legs, gray combat boots are stuck on my feet,
and a black camisole covers my torso. I tuck away my green dress

quietly since I had no chance to do it earlier.

I barge out of the bathroom and into the bedroom and say loudly, "We need to go to Kieling."

The group huddles around me, all asking the same question: "Why?"

"We need to get information. Kieling is part of the prophecy." I notice that Natalia cleaned up the blood on the carpet from my forehead.

"Yes, we can ask them about the moonstone. And about the prophecy," Fiomi suggests.

"They won't know anything about it," Natalia says. "We didn't. Fiomi didn't. And Fiomi's parents get the newspaper every morning!"

"It's the Divyeine newspaper," Ian says. "They won't send it out to the other tribes."

"It doesn't matter," Fiomi says. "I know Kieling. They'll figure it out."

I look at Ian. He gazes wistfully back at me and forces a smile. He turns around and gulps, his Adam's apple bobbing like a buoy in a rough current. I can see his dread, his trepidation. He's waiting for something to happen. I can smell it: the smell of sour, rotten loss. He's going to lose something. But I don't know what.

What I do know is that what he's going to lose isn't something good.

FOURTEEN

WE PACK QUICKLY AND HEAD OUT, not bothering to be quiet. Natalia's parents left an hour ago to run errands and go to work and whatnot. I had to change my clothes; Natalia did not approve of what I was wearing. Too obvious that I am from Divyeine, she said. She said I'd give myself away. So with my own clothes packed snugly in my backpack, which is more like a potato sack or a knapsack, we trudge on to the border, moving quickly. I don't know how this bright blue, sparkly, iridescent denim skirt and striped purple and blue crop top doesn't stand out. Huh, I'm in Meliandor. What do I expect?

I have never seen the Willow tree in the sunlight before. The only time I would go was at night when I would meet up with Ian. The moon was the only source of energy I could rely on for light. The Willow tree stands tall. Its long tendrils flourish with healthy leaves that glow green. Flowers have begun to sprout in the grass, growing high and bright. Petals layer the ground in a thick blanket. No matter how strong my outer layer is, I always love seeing the flowers bloom.

FIFTEEN

KIELING IS NOT WHAT I EXPECTED. Getting through to the tribe was easy enough. I expected retina scanners and a well-built base coded with mechanisms to keep people who are not from Kieling out. Instead, no one stands in front of the iron gates coated with a thick layer of white paint that loom in front of us. There are no retina scanners, no ID scanners, nothing. The gates are even unlocked, and a steel sign etched with the words "Welcome to Kieling" is plastered to the column that holds up the left gate.

Fiomi and I exchange a glance; Fiomi senses my worry, but she just nods. This really is Kieling. Nothing is wrong. There are two paths: one that leads to the community of Kieling behind the main building and one that leads to the main building itself. The five of us tread down the left white path that leads to the main building, where all the officials stay.

The main building is enormous and intricate. Gray pillars glittering with silver embedded in the sides shoot up from the ground, and turrets form rooms five stories above the floor. The entrance consists of two dull-colored steel doors and glass. Lots of glass. Large panels of windows cover most of the sides of the building. Warm white light glimmers from a modern chandelier hanging from a part of the roof extended from the front door to provide a bit of shelter.

Levie balls his fist and raps at the door. Once, twice, three times. Three sharp knocks that reverberate across the large, enclosed area. Fiomi pushes her fingers to lower his fist.

"You don't need to knock in Kieling," she says quietly. "They can already see you."

"That's creepy!" Ian says with uneasiness.

"It's fine," Fiomi says. "I live here."

Our mouths gape open in surprise. "You live . . . here?! Of course! You're Zesten Bianco's daughter! How could we be so ignorant?" I say, mouth ajar. Zesten Bianco is the leader of Kieling. I had forgotten that, since in Divyeine we spent more time doing physical training than learning about the tribes, but now that I stand here in Kieling, the memories come back. Natalia just stands with her arms crossed, her smiling expression showing something like, *Yeah, my friend is really cool, and I already knew that.*

Suddenly, the doors boom open slowly, creaking and scratching and eventually falling into place against the walls. A tall man stands in front of us, his posture straight, his hands clasped behind his back. The man holds his head high and sticks his nose in the air. He carries himself in a way that makes me think he is proud. Proud of himself, proud of his work. He glances at us through his silver-rimmed glasses. His clean-shaven face softens when he sees Fiomi.

"Papa!" Fiomi says brightly, rushing into his open arms. He sinks to the floor and squeezes her tight. A woman emerges from the building, her hair a flame streaked with silver strands. She places her hand on her husband's shoulder and smiles down at her daughter, wrinkles forming around her eyes. Zesten and Faye Bianco. The couple who help run Kieling. I'm speechless, yet I'm so excited to speak with them.

"Esme!" Faye says with delight. "It's wonderful to see you, daughter!"

Fiomi's eyes travel to her mother's face. "What?"

SIXTEEN

THE WOMAN COCKS HER HEAD, looking confused. "What is it, daughter?"

Fiomi walks toward the woman slowly. "Mama, my name isn't Esme."

"Of course it is! I named you."

"Honey," Zesten says gently, "Her name is Fiomi. You named her Fiomi."

"I don't remember that!" Fiomi's mother says haughtily. She turns, and I can hear the clacks of her high heels on the marble floor, which eventually recede into awkward silence.

"Come in," Fiomi's father says to us. "We must talk."

We walk in through the grand hallway, which doesn't really seem that majestic but is elegant in a modern way: the looks of wood, steel, and lots of white. Zesten leads us through the hallway into a sitting area with a couple chairs and heavily stuffed poufs. We settle down on what's available, Zesten seating himself in a blue velvet chair.

"What happened to Mama, Papa?"

"Let us talk about the moonstone first. It'll give you some backstory for what happened to your mother," he says calmly.

"The moonstone?"

"The moonstone!" I blurt. "The moonstone!" I'm excited because I connected it with the prophecy. Zesten looks at me. "Sorry!"

"No, you're correct. The Kieling moonstone. Our treasure."

"Your treasure?" Levie asks.

"The treasure is our moonstone. The moonstone is very important in the Kieling culture. We worship the moonstone, and it grants us intelligence."

"So you would be dumb if you didn't have it?" Ian asks.

I smack him. "That's rude!" I whisper-yell in his ear.

He shrugs. "I was asking a valid question."

"To answer your question, boy—"

"Ian."

"Ian. We would still have our intelligence. The moonstone is just a belief, really. That's actually why your mother has gone berserk, Fiomi. She fell so deeply for the lie that she thinks differently now. That without the moonstone, she can't think. It's as if when the moonstone was lost, part of her soul was lost too. Of course, what happened is psychological, but the whole situation is very strange." Zesten folds his arms and leans back in his blue velvet chair. He crosses his legs.

"Oh," Ian says.

"But the moonstone is Divyeine's, sir," I say, speaking as politely as I can.

"Yes, well, it is ours as well. It is not only Divyeine's prized possession, it is also ours."

We erupt into questions. "How?" "What in the world are you talking about?" "Why is the moonstone so important?" "Do you have any food?"

"Did you seriously just ask if there was food?" I say in disgust toward Ian.

He looks at me. "Yes. I'm hungry," he whines.

Zesten rings for a servant, who comes and goes with a wave of Zesten's hand after Zesten asks for a snack.

The servant comes back carrying a silver platter of food and drinks on her hand. She sets it on the coffee table obediently and shuffles out of the room, leaving us with privacy. Ian reaches his hand out to a teacup. He raises it to his lips and takes a sip.

"The moonstone was originally Divyeine's, yes, but we borrowed it to study it, and it's been with us ever since. We've grown to love it, to worship it. We aren't even studying it anymore. We were using it because of our superstition, but we don't know where it is. They are asking for it back, but we can't give it back because we lost it," Zesten says.

"We need to show you the prophecy." The five of us exchange nods before handing the paper I retrieved from my bag to Zesten. "Before you read, please tell us what happened to the moonstone."

Zesten's face hardens. "It was taken to the labs on the other side of the Border. There, they studied it. The labs there are the best we've got. They found something about the moonstone."

"What did they find?" we ask.

"They found that whoever has it is able to rule the world."

My friends turn to look at me. "Did you know about this?" Fiomi asks.

"N-no!" I stammer. "Never!" A foul, cold feeling takes over me, and the hairs on my neck stand up. Why does it seem like we all have something to hide?

SEVENTEEN

ZESTEN STANDS UP. "You're from Divyeine?"

I hang my head low. "Yes, sir."

Zesten glares at me. His clear green eyes exude an unnamed emotion. "I think you should leave."

He clenches the back of his blue armchair tightly, his knuckles whitening.

"Get this girl out of my house," he says icily to the servant, who emerges from the door quietly. My friends spring up and out of their poufs.

"Micah," Fiomi warns.

There are only two reasons why he would want me to leave. One, because he knows that I cannot leave Divyeine and interact with people from other tribes. That might be the case, especially since he, the head of Kieling, should be firm about following the rules. But the way he talked and how he looked at me makes me think differently. Two, because he believes I'm dangerous and that now that I know everything, I can help Divyeine destroy him because they kept the moonstone and weren't even studying it.

The servant leads me out of the house.

I follow the servant, actually glad to leave Kieling. She brings me outside the front gate and locks me out of Kieling. My eyes follow her back to the massive building, where she then retreats into a side door. Kieling is no longer asking for visitors. They're asking for war.

EIGHTEEN

I COUNT THE SECONDS TICKING BY, each feeling like a minute, an hour, a day. No one comes outside, so I'm left alone. There's a slight breeze, and I'm only covered by a thin cardigan Natalia gave me. Natalia was sweet to give me clothes, but honestly, I'm starting to really hate this outfit. It reeks of Meliandor.

With nothing to do, I rummage through my backpack and take out the photograph. Part of the image is ripped from pressure in my bag. Now that I think about it, my backpack is cutting into my shoulder, and my shoulder aches. I slide it off and set it next to me on the gravel-filled ground.

The picture doesn't hold the brightness of both our smiles anymore. It's faded, dull. Just like our friendship. We need to keep our friendship. I already lost him once. I can't lose him again. Things have changed. We have changed since we last met. It isn't the same as it was, but we had such a strong bond with each other. He was the light during the darkness of my rough childhood, and he was gone, and now he's back, so I can't just let him go that easily.

I hear footsteps, and I turn around to find the four others behind the bars of the gate.

Fiomi reaches out to me, her fingers outstretched. I take her hand. "Hey," she says. "My papa told us things I think you need to know."

"Can you do it when you're here?" I say.

Fiomi smashes her hand against the button that opens the gates. I move out of the way and let the mechanism do its work. My friends run through the opening, the gate closing behind them, and everyone except Fiomi wraps me in a hug. Why?

"We need to talk," Fiomi says.

We walk away. Away from the closed gates of Kieling. Away from our friends. I'm getting the itching feeling that I just need to go. I need to go somewhere to think. To talk, to myself mostly. I need someplace enclosed, hidden. A secluded place that forms a barrier around my thoughts, a wall against humanity and the real world.

We walk for a mile or two. Why we are walking so far away,

I'm clueless, and Fiomi tells me. "Papa can't hear this. He can't see that I'm talking to you. Let me tell you why."

"Go on," I say, folding my arms across my chest and tapping my foot on the ground, now filled with dusty dirt instead of gravel. We walked very far.

"Divyeine had the moonstone first. They knew how valuable it was. That small stone is worth a lot of money. Kieling was interested in the moonstone. All the tribes know about the Divyeine moonstone. What they didn't know was that Kieling took it to study it. Then they found out the secret about the moonstone. And they couldn't give it back because of the belief, but also because of the value of the moonstone. So Divyeine started to get angry. One, because they didn't get their moonstone back, and two, because they knew Kieling wanted the money, the power. Papa knew they were getting angry, and he decided to do the right thing and give the moonstone back, but when he contacted the people working in the labs, they reported that the moonstone was gone. At meetings with the other tribes, Papa could sense the anger coming from Divyeine. He has been suspecting Divyeine would do something bad, but now that he has seen the prophecy, he fears that the prophecy may actually be real. That's why he doesn't want me talking to you."

I understand now. Divyeine is dangerous. Any small step and you die. But Kieling is the same way. They're dangerous, too. Danger looms in their presence. Their power is not their physical strength. It's their minds. It's their cunning ideas and sly thoughts. They can't fight sword to sword, but they can go to war. And now I know that's exactly what they're planning to do.

NINETEEN

DEATH IS HOW DIVYEINE PLANS TO TAKE OUT THE OTHER TRIBES. They won't let anything get in their way. They are ready. I am not. I can't switch tribes. But I wish I left a long time ago. I wish I did when I met Ian at the border. When he was about to tell me something. When I felt like I really loved him for who he was. I wanted to tell him I loved him, but that love was stupid. I was only seven. I was young, naive, and whole. Perfect. Before I broke. Psychologically and physically. In a way, I'm glad my mother punched my nose. I'm glad I didn't see Ian until the party. Looking back, I don't think I would have wanted him to see me in such rough shape. Besides, I wouldn't have met Natalia. Or Fiomi. Or Levie. Oh, Levie. There is no clue to why I like him. I just do.

Fiomi and I walk in indefinite silence. We walk half the way back because the other three are already waiting for us away from the Kieling grounds.

"We can't go back to Meliandor, I'm sorry," Natalia says quietly. None of us ask her why, she just tells us. "My parents said they had to go on a work trip for a starter fashion company. They told me I have to stay with a friend."

All of us exchange glances. "Let's just keep walking," I say, my words running with exhaustion. "We can stop once we are completely away from Kieling's grounds."

We agree and continue trudging up the trail. As we are walking deeper within the knitted trees forming a sort of forest, I sense a sudden humidity. The air is thick with water vapor, and it is making me feel dizzy and disgustingly grimy.

"I need somewhere to wash up," I say, and we all look at Levie. He is our only option, but we know we won't be able to stay at his house. We've already walked deep into the forest, and Kieling is the farthest place someone could get from Semberic.

"I'm sure we'll find somewhere to clean up," Fiomi says reassuringly. "I know these woods well. There's a waterfall and a few cabins near here, I believe."

A small flame sparks hope. A little kindling that will soon rise to be a big fire. We walk through the wooded area, being careful where we walk—the ground is uneven, and roots lie thick on the mossy green floor, so we could trip on a tree's foot. We walk for what feels like hours, and eventually, we move into a clearing.

Bright light pushes its way through the canopy of leaves that lie like a blanket on the surface of the tall trees. Fiomi was right—there it is. Clear blue water tumbles down, crashing and sloshing in a roaring waterfall. Green grass and smooth stones litter the ground. Baby daisies pop up here and there. Fiomi was true to her word. Next to the waterfall, three oak-wood cabins sit peacefully.

"Oh! I call a cabin! Seriously, I would like to share, but like, I need the privacy!" Natalia shouts.

I laugh. "Sure," I say, "As long as I'm in the cabin nearest the waterfall. Fiomi, I can stay with you."

Ian opens and closes his mouth. He yearns to say something. I let him.

"Ian?"

"What?" he asks.

"Go ahead."

He gets the notion and sighs. "I kind of wanted to sleep in your cabin."

I tilt my head so my vision is pointed at my shoes. I pause, then say uncomfortably, "Do you really want to?"

"I want to talk."

"Then talk!" I laugh sharply. "I'm going to bathe in the pool."
The pool forms in a deep valley where the waterfall flows. Gallons upon gallons of clear turquoise water fill this narrow bowl, creating a pool. I trek to the cabin nearest the waterfall and go inside. It's new and modern like Kieling, but a layer of dust sits on the floor, and more dust particles climb on each other, pushing and shoving and swirling in the air. Someone from Kieling most likely made these cabins and forgot about them. It seems that no one has used them in a very long time.

I strip off my ugly shirt and gross acid-washed skirt and return to my normal self, using my camisole and a pair of running shorts I found in my backpack as swimwear. My backpack has my jade green dress from the party stuffed into it carelessly. I never want to see that Meliandor outfit again. I'm never going to wear it again, but I just stuff it back in my bag.

I walk out, ecstatic to feel the sunshine on my bare skin. I sink my toes in the shallow end of the pool. The scenery out here seems so natural, but the only genuinely real thing in this society is the Willow. Everything in our society is human-made, which is why sometimes things in Auneaire might seem so surreal or perfect. The water is warm. The heat of the sun is blazing, but the water balances it out. The weather is gorgeous, with blue skies and small pillowy clouds floating around evenly. I swim to the waterfall and feel the cold water beating down on me. I suck in a breath and sink underneath, small bubbles popping at the surface. It isn't long before I touch the bottom, which is smooth, clean, and not far from the surface, maybe just four feet or so.

I enjoy meditating. It helps me focus on myself, my mind. It grounds me and reassures me that I have arrived in this time on a time train that moves quickly toward a destination that isn't real—it never ends. The train goes around in a loop, and that's probably how we get deja vu. I should only focus on this moment. I should be careful, and wary. I need to be removed of my infinite thinking and loud imagination, which keep pushing into my mind.

I float to the surface, my lungs still filled with air, and exhale. Then inhale. I float to a calmer part of the bowl, away from the falling water. But the calmer part of the pool isn't calm anymore. It splashes and sloshes, and a sun-basted Levie slips down to sit next to me as I cling to the rocky bank. We are sitting next to each other, closely. Discomfort invades my stomach, fleeting, quickly moving away—no, getting shoved away by another feeling. A feeling I'm moderately unfamiliar with, but I'm prepared, I'm eager, I'm compelled to push forward and invite back into my emotions bank. This feeling isn't new to me, but I've only felt it once in my life, when I was young, when I had Ian. I definitely believed I would sometimes forget the feeling, but it's what I want, what I yearn for. And that's exactly what it is. Desire.

TWENTY

MY CHEST IS BURNING. My heart is thumping. I can feel my molecules buzzing with frenzy. I turn to Levie. I can't help it. I'm seeing him in a brighter light, a clearer vision. He's just so beautiful. His golden blond hair is brushed to the side, and his eyes are as blue and clear as the pool. His lips are pink and full, his tanned torso bare. His muscles are curved and vividly indented, dark and completely outlined. He's staring at me. Ian is sitting on a rock, looking in our direction—most likely at me. Fiomi and Natalia are turned away from us, so I can see only their backs.

I can't help it. I know it's not right. I know I haven't known Levie for long, but I can't help it. I can't help it.

I lean forward and meet his lips with mine. Levie tenses, and his eyes widen in surprise, becoming big ovals. It's not long before his shoulders drop, and he takes his trembling hand to caress my cheek, to steady himself, maybe both, but he leaves it there. His long fingers snake through my hair, and his lips are still pressed to mine. We're sharing our air, we're sharing this moment, we're letting happiness take us away. I realize I'm really giving Levie my all. And he's giving me his.

TWENTY-ONE

IAN IS NOT HAPPY. His arms are crossed, and his green-hazel eyes are flecked with specks of fire. He's so angry. We're standing on the rocks near the edge of the pool. My hair is still damp from swimming.

He throws his hands up in exasperation. "What the hell, Micah?"

"What?" I say, taking a step away.

"You can't just kiss some random boy!"

"I did not! He's not random," I argue. "Besides, it's not for you to decide!"

"You can't kiss him . . ."

"Why?" I glower at him, speaking through gritted teeth.

"Not after . . ." I finish his sentence. Not after he professed to me. Not after I kissed him.

I sigh and direct my eyes to his hands, which are curled into tight fists. "I'm sorry I hurt you with my actions. But it's my life. Not yours."

My words are reverberating in his mind, replaying over and over. He's trying to make sense of what I just said. Then it hits him, and his face softens. I expected the opposite.

"I'm sorry," he apologizes. He presses his warm palm to my cheek and pulls me into his chest, where we embrace each other gently, our bodies sealed together. I pull away.

"I can't do this," I breathe. It's too complicated. Too new. I'm not used to what I'm feeling and what is happening right now. I'm not used to the once-familiar feeling of Ian's hand on my cheek or the newness of Levie's lips on mine. So I run into my cabin, I bury my face into my pillow, and even though it's still afternoon and the sun is still out, I will myself to fall asleep. And I do.

TWENTY-TWO

I SLEEP UNTIL NOON THE NEXT DAY. The past few days were not kind enough to give me all the sleep I needed, and today God finally granted my wish for a good rest. Fiomi is still sleeping. I look outside my window to the other cabin, where I can spot Ian curled up on the top bunk. I tiptoe outside and peek my head into the boys' cabin. Both are out cold, exhausted from the past few days. Then I sneak to Natalia's cabin to see how she is doing.

Natalia is tucked under her crimson bedsheets. I do a double take—when did Natalia get to bring her own colorful bedsheets? There is no way she fit them into her backpack. Oddly enough, the bedsheets look like the ones I found in my cabin and shared with her—only red. I creep to Natalia and touch the pads of my fingers against the sheets. They are moist, damp, and weirdly warm. I withdraw my hand, and my stomach drops when I smell a horrible stench. An iron stench, to be exact. Terrified, I look at my fingers and gag, stumbling away from Natalia's body. They are red with sticky blood. Two points connect, and I fumble to remove the top sheet from Natalia's body, revealing a deep bloody gash in her throat.

I press my hands to her chest, searching for life. Nothing. I press my fingers to her wrist, seeking the faint thump of a heartbeat. There is no pulse. I drop her hand, limp and cold, and let out a panicked cry for help.

Ian and Levie scramble in, still coping with fatigue, but they snap awake as soon as they see Natalia.

"Holy crap!" Ian shouts with disbelief. I don't get why crap is holy.

"Natalia!" Levie says. He looks at me wildly. "What happened?" he shudders.

I'm unable to answer. I'm trying to figure out that question myself.

"Did you search for a pulse?" Levie cries hurriedly. I nod quickly.

"I was just checking on everybody when I found her!"

"Oh my gosh!" Levie yells. "What are we going to tell Fiomi?"

TWENTY-THREE

THERE IS NO WAY THAT FIOMI DOESN'T HEAR OUR CRIES. Our cries are too horrified for her not to wake up and investigate. Like I expected, she appears in the doorway to see what's going on, sees Natalia, and crumples to the floor like a rag doll.

"Natalia," she sobs, wrapping her arms around her pale legs and burying her face into her knees. "What happened?" she bawls, squeezing her eyes shut. Strands of her messy, fiery hair fall onto her face, sticking to her tear-struck cheeks.

"Damn it!" she screams. "She's not dead. She's not dead. She's not dead!" Fiomi crawls over to me and grips my arm. She's in bad shape. She's freaked out. She can't believe this is happening. I think this is the first stage of closure.

Fiomi moves through this stage quickly. The next stage is harder to bear. Fiomi is bouncing around, rocking back and forth, clenching her sides, and emitting gut-wrenching howls of pain. Inside pain. She's not all right.

A sharp knock on the closed cabin door sounds. Ian and I eye each other, sharing the same thought: who's there?

I get up, make my way to the door, and cautiously open it, the door creaking slowly. The person who stands outside is a girl. A girl I don't know.

"Excuse me," she says. "We heard screams. Is there a problem?"

"We?" I ask, my eyes trailing her up and down. She's slim and impeccably beautiful. Her body is covered by a short, thin layer of black satin fabric held up by two spaghetti straps.

"Oh, yes, us." She moves aside to reveal four people waiting behind her. "May we come in?"

"No," I say, faking a quick smile. "We've had a bit of a problem here, and my friend needs space."

The girl wasn't asking for an answer. She pushes her way through Levie, Ian, and me, and stops dead to gape at Fiomi and Natalia. "The hell?" she says with an open mouth. It seems so fake, like it's not genuine surprise.

"Yeah," I growl. "She's dead. And none of us did it."

TWENTY-FOUR

"WHY'D YOU KILL HER?" Levie says angrily at no one in particular, but most likely meaning one of the boys in the group. The group is silent with gaping mouths.

"I don't even know you!" one of the boys says. He looks a lot like the girl in the front.

"Then let's go into another cabin and explain," Levie says.

I'm relieved we're taking this to another room. One more minute and I think I might've gotten really sick from looking at Natalia's dead body. I didn't want to look, but it was hard to turn away.

The other group of five stands tensely near the bunks, so my friends and I sit near the doorway. Levie sits next to Ian, who sits next to me. Fiomi stands behind us, leaning on the doorway. It's like Levie forgot what happened between us. Boys always forget.

Ian forgot. Now so did Levie. I should know that by now. The group of five squish together on the bunk bed.

The boy says, "I'm Foster. This is Farrah. We're twins." He acknowledges the girl to his left, the rude one, the gorgeous one. I notice that they really do look alike. They meet my eyes with both of their gleaming caramel ones.

The other two boys stand up to shake my hand. I don't give it to them. Awkwardly, they retract their hands.

One of the boys, who has curly brown hair, speaks. "I'm Denzel," he says. He has smooth, dark brown skin, and his voice is like honey.

"My name is Luz," the other boy says, his voice so much deeper than Denzel's. Luz smiles at me with his coal black eyes. He has olive skin and a mass of shiny jet-black hair draped across his scalp like a mop.

There is one more girl. She sits behind Luz, her fingers wrapped around his shoulders. Her face is sprinkled with freckles, and her green glasses are pushed up the bridge of her pale nose, sparking light in her emerald eyes. Her honey brown hair is tied in a knot. She doesn't speak, and she doesn't say her name. A gasp sounds from behind me.

"Dec?"

TWENTY-FIVE

THE GIRL'S NAME IS DEC, I suppose. I wonder if it's a nickname of sorts. Dec slides out of the bed and stops. Stares. Not at me, but at the source of the throaty whisper. I swivel my head to find Fiomi staring at Dec.

"Fiomi," Dec breathes, her eyes catching flame.

"Reedecsee." Fiomi wipes her eyes of tears and looks at Dec hard. So, her full name must be Reedecsee. There is a coldness to Fiomi's voice I've never heard before because it's coming from the sweetest girl I know. She clenches her hand and bites her lip. If looks could kill . . . Why is their relationship so unsteady?

"Father told you not to come back," Fiomi spits bitterly.

"I didn't." Reedecsee snorts. "And I hope I never will, ex-step-sister." Oh. That's why they hate each other. The whole fiasco of how Zesten Bianco and Faye, his wife and Fiomi's mother, divorced so Zesten could follow his heart and marry Gabrielle Garmond. However, staying with such an intense woman snapped Zesten out of his little love trance and drove him to divorce Gabrielle and run back to Faye, the woman he truly loved. Once Zesten remarried Faye, Gabrielle was both angered and embarrassed and ended up raising her daughter, who I now learn is Reedecsee, alone.

"You're here." Fiomi seethes. "These woods are too close to Kieling. You know that." Reedecsee just shrugs. Her words make sense. The woods are obscured from the world but also in plain sight. We're together but alone. We're concealed but can be found. This isn't a matter of hide-and-seek, though. This is a matter of life and death.

TWENTY-SIX

I CAN'T BREATHE. I smooth my hair back, so it falls behind my shoulders, and open the door to get fresh air. Denzel follows me.

"Hey. You 'kay?" he says, biting the inside of his cheek.

"I guess," I reply, my gaze locked on the purple sky.

"Needed some air?"

I roll my eyes. "Isn't it obvious?" Denzel laughs, a full, hearty noise that makes my head hurt.

"What do you want?" I sigh. He's looking at me expectantly, searching for something, an answer in my facial expression, studying the morose emotion playing on my face.

"Why are you here?" he says.

"Because there's something we need to finish. Something is starting, and we need to end it."

"Huh," Denzel says thoughtfully. "Surprisingly, we're up to

something similar."

My brows knit together. I fixate my gaze into Denzel's eyes. "What are you doing?" I ask curiously, chewing on my lower lip.

"Oh." Denzel chuckles. "We're going to end a war."

TWENTY-SEVEN

I GAWP, shocked. "What?"

"Sorry," Denzel apologizes. "It sounds stupid, I know. Something about an idiot prophecy. 'Ster was going crazy about it."

"Ster?" I peep, still frozen with disbelief.

"Foster. Sometimes my tongue goes wild. Pretty stupid, considering I always have to talk." If Foster was the one who wanted to follow it, he must be in Divyeine, which means that Farrah is as well. I don't recognize them, but because Divyeine has around twice the population and land area as the other tribes, I don't know everyone.

"Talaskin?" I guess.

Denzel winks at me. "You got it!"

"So you guys are the five leaders?"

The muscles in Denzel's jaw harden. "I..." Denzel says slowly.

"I wish we weren't." He's choosing his words carefully.

I cock my head. "Why?" I say innocently.

"Because I can't do it!" Denzel yells. "I can't end a war! That's what Divyeine's supposed to do, though they are the ones starting it. Besides, I don't know how we are supposed to go across into Divyeine! Foster and Farrah aren't fond of their parents."

"It's okay," I coax. "You don't have to end a war."

Denzel's brow furrows. "I don't have to?" he murmurs, puzzled.

"You don't," I say gently. This is my prophecy. I want to do it. We were all together until Natalia was brutally murdered. We were all together, and now we're not. But we need to stick together. Or else the walls will crumble. The sky will shake, and we will meet our defeat.

Will they complete the prophecy or meet their defeat? That's what the prophecy said. Three of us are bound to die. More, if we don't stop this. I can't let that happen. Though, prophecies aren't always true … right?

TWENTY-EIGHT

WE NEED TO GET THIS CLEARED UP. I barge into the cabin and peer at the seven other people in the room. Seven, plus me and Denzel. Nine. Four more than the five leaders. Five more than the four leaders. The original leaders. The ones who already completed part of their journey. The ones who already lost one player. One player in a game bigger than her. A game bigger and better and harder to win. A game that can play you.

"When did you start?" I clasp my hands behind my back and look hard at the four other new leaders. The four other older leaders. It is not possible that having one of us die after taking our roles as the five leaders is a coincidence. That means we are the leaders, right? If they started later than us, and if one of them hasn't died yet, then that means we are the leaders.

"What?" Farrah scowls. "What in the world are you talking

about?"

"When did you start?" I say, my voice cracking. "You haven't lost a player yet. There's five of you."

"Hey, hey," Denzel says, hands up. "No need to get upset." He backs toward his group and stands protectively in front of them.

"When did you start?" I say, my voice shaking with anger. I curl my hands into fists.

"I don't understand," Luz says, his words slurred as he shakes his head. Larveson. Luz is from Larveson.

"I do," I say in a low, dangerous voice. I snap. "You're not the leaders! You aren't now, and you never will be."

The fear in their eyes is approaching mine. What am I turning into? My mother? I can't turn into my mother. She hurt me enough. I don't want to hurt them, but I already did. This is something I'm so set on, and even though I claimed the role of a leader as my own, I feel so attached to it already that it's making me angry. Maybe it's just the ominous darkness of the prophecy and knowing that someone I just met was murdered in cold blood, which follows the prophecy. Maybe it's just Natalia's death getting to me.

Levie stares at me, his blue eyes piercing my heart. "Get out," he says.

"What?"

"Get out, Micah. Take a breather. Calm down. Drink some water in the bucket, the one in my cabin. It's from the waterfall. I put iodine in it."

I nod mutely at Levie's statement, trying to find an argument that could withstand his icy words, only to find that I agree with him. I needed to get away, and I didn't get that chance. I can't stay here while Natalia's body just rots. Levie should do something. He's from Semberic, after all. I glance back at Fiomi, with her ragged, lonely appearance, huddled in the corner alone.

I sweep myself out of the room, pleased to be alone. I try to run, to get my heart rate up and to gain the rushed feelings of content and calm, but all I earn are weights, metal bars that glue my feet to the rocky ground, and sacks of concrete that lie on my back, making my shoulders hunch forward. Not literally, but I feel them there. This wasn't the refreshment I needed, but it's refreshment nonetheless.

TWENTY-NINE

I TIE MY HAIR BACK TO GET IT AWAY FROM MY FACE. This is going to be some hard work. I have sanitary products in my backpack, so I retrieve a pair of powder blue latex gloves and slap them on. I move carefully. The body is so daunting, lying there. *Come get me*, it taunts. I'm ready for you, dead body. It's fine. I stretch toward it slowly, a rotting smell reaching my nose. I lug the body out from the cabin, looking away from the distinct red maculation of blood, sucking in oxygen through my mouth, trying to relieve myself of the horrible stench. I drag the body down to a thicket. The space between each tree is so small that the tall trees are practically grappling each other for space, uprooting each long limb, each curling finger of a root. I doubt anything or anyone would dare come close to this spot if they knew about the poor girl.

I was so very wrong about being ready. Seeing poor Natalia,

her face slack, makes my stomach flip. I would vomit, but I haven't eaten anything since the meeting with Fiomi's father, Zesten.

I don't have the materials to give her a proper burial. I have no shovel or any supplies that would help me dig deep enough to appropriately bury a body. I shake my head. I should stop referring to her as "a body." She was just recently alive, and my friend. I probably shouldn't have dragged her, it was cruel. I find some wildflowers in the grass near the trees. I pick them and bring them back to Natalia. A wave of guilt washes over me as I crouch next to her. How could I let this happen? And to be so careless with the body of the girl who was once my friend. I brush off the dirt from her face and place her hands on her stomach, where I set down the flowers I found.

My stomach growls, scratching my insides scathingly. It feels wrong of me to search for food after I just dealt with the dead body of my friend, but I need to eat. I walk to the pool, my bare toes curling in the soft blades of grass that sit silently next to the burst of the waterfall. I rip off my shirt, tying it and knotting it so it resembles some sort of net or bag. The shirt isn't actually mine— it's Ian's. I may or may not have stolen it from his duffel bag before I went to sleep yesterday. I squat and swish my shirt filled with worms I dug up from the grassy soil in the pool, feeling certain I will catch a fish. I sit, waiting.

I fail to understand what I'm doing wrong. I'm so erroneous in all my thoughts. Frustrated, I thrust my dripping dark shirt, still filled with worms, to the ground. The ground almost seems to bend around the shirt, hugging it slightly.

I touch my fingers to the coarse soil and whisper, "Thank you."

Thank you for being the only one who really listens without turning away. Thank you for knowing my mistakes. Thank you for being so sweet. I'm sorry for staining your ground with blood. Although it's really not my fault, and I'm not sure whose it is.

THIRTY

I'M GETTING REALLY HUNGRY, so I dive into the low pool, feeling the frigid water catch my body in its embrace as I crash through its surface. Small fish zip at the bottom through moss and seaweed growing on the pool floor, their iridescent scales glimmering from the sunlight that shines through the clear water.

I love the water. I always have. It brings back memories I adore. The first time I went swimming was when I was five. I was already training for combat, fighting, and being aggressive. Now, because of that and my parents, violence is my nature. I wish it wasn't, but I've wished too many times and know that wishes don't come true. Anyway, I was last in my class. Last place all the time. But there was my teacher, a general named Chris Calowell.

General Calowell had seen many things. He had fought in the war that broke our world but also fixed it. This war screamed, Look *at this! Look at what war does to us! Do you really want it?* That's when everyone snapped out of it. Calowell did too. He wasn't able to fight anyway. In the war, shrapnel damaged his left femur. He didn't recover well. Calowell was like me. Suffering from post-traumatic stress disorder, he couldn't erase the image of war from his mind. But we found a way to help each other. He taught me how to be strong. To be ready. To use violence as a last resort and to find another way. He became softer, gentler, the small chinks in his armor growing bigger and wider until they engulfed him in layers of kindness. He seemed to have become a different person entirely. This progressed slowly, over the course of a year, and by the time I turned six, Calowell had completely transformed into a new man. But I didn't forget that he still lived in Divyeine. And he was a general. Only weeks after his transformation, he was shipped away to go fight at the Border. Even with his bad femur. Divyeine doesn't care if you're hurt or not. They need all the people they can muster.

This Border not many people tend to talk about. This Border is not the border between each of the tribes. It is the Border encircling us all, forming a barrier between us and the rest of the world. This is the Border. With a capital B.

Auneaire is our society. But outside Auneaire lies so much

more than I've ever known, and ever will know. At least, that's what I imagine. All the tribes are my world, and everyone else's. No one has ever been outside the Border. No one is allowed to— well, except the top soldiers. No one knows what lies away from us, across the vast ocean that encircles all our land and more. Or at least, no one who hasn't fought in a war there. But that doesn't count because whoever goes to the Border never comes back.

I'm not extremely talented, probably because I never really aspired to be a soldier, or a fighter. I'm strong, and I could probably work to be the top of my class or a top soldier if I wanted to, but I don't. It's just not who I am. I could have dedicated my heart if I wanted to, but I didn't. Yes, I am interested to see what lies past the wall, but there are so many stories about the Border that scare me.

Calowell fought at the Border. He saw things he should not have seen. His post-traumatic stress disorder became more severe. He developed a vehement longing for pain. It drove him crazy. To wrap it up, he killed himself. That's what he did. He wasn't able to cope. That's what Divyeine told me. He needed me. The one thing he needed the most was something so far away, and it wasn't the distance between us that drove him insane, it was the knowledge that even if I was with him, I wouldn't be able to help him at all.

I'm not letting all that we taught each other go to waste. Natalia's death was a turning point for me, and I'm determined to figure out who her killer is.

THIRTY-ONE

I'VE CAUGHT A FISH. I wasn't even thinking about it; I just threw my hands out, and one happened to curl around a fish. A rather large fish too. The fish squirms and struggles in my hand, its scales slippery, but I don't let go. I find a way to hoist myself out of the pool and let the fish squirm in my hand. I don't want to do anything else to hurt it, but it's probably best for it to die quickly. I pick up a rock from the grass and drive it into its head. I set it down on a smooth, flat rock near the waterfall, the stone hot from the sun's energy. I pay no attention to the shirt that lies there, worms still inching across the fabric.

I'm soaking wet in my tank top and shorts, so I lie next to the fish, relaxing on the warm rock against which I press my back. I close my eyes, feeling the bare skin of my legs tingle with pleasure from the heat.

After a while, I trudge back to Levie's cabin, where I had left my backpack. I find a cup settled next to the bucket of water Levie had mentioned. I fill it with water and bring it to my lips. The taste is refreshing and sweet. Usually water doesn't have a flavor, but this water is something different. Everything here is so different, so cloying, so sickeningly sweet that it seems unreal.

I move back outside and find a patchy area of dirt. I use what resources I can to build a sort of campfire so the fire doesn't spread. I learned this in training when I was younger. I know how to make a fire. So I use what I know. This is where I need it. I rub two dry sticks together hard, vigorously spinning the sticks in my fingers. I can feel the growing heat, the energy, the molecules buzzing with excitement. Then, the end of the sticks catches fire. Amazed, I stare at the flame, so bright and beautiful, watching it dance and play, teasing the grass near it. The patch of grass recoils and wilts, turning itself into a small ball of acrid, smoldering blades. I move to the rock again and put down the sticks of fire, feeding twigs to the flames. It's definitely unsanitary to use a random stick to skewer my fish, but I hope the bacteria will die once I cook it. Levie comes out of the cabin, done with the heated chat that raged inside. He walks to the rock, where he smiles loosely and sits himself down next to me.

"I'm sorry," he apologizes.

I quirk him a fast, tight upturn of my lips and say, "For what?"

"For acting like a jerk." He sighs, lifting his head. We lock eyes for a moment, Levie staring intently at me. I receive the message. We both know what he's sorry for. I'm sorry too.

"That was unexpected," I say. "I'm the one who should be apologizing." He laughs.

"Yeah, well, I definitely wasn't expecting that, I promise you."

I lean into him, and he wraps his arms around me comfortingly. We stare at the blazing flame in front of us. I turn the fish over the fire. It doesn't take as long as I expected for it to cook, so I take the skewered fish and stomp out the fire. I hold it away from me because it is still hot and wait for the fire to die down before I place it back on the rocks to cool.

"I caught a fish," I say smugly.

"I can very well see that," Levie jokes, pulling me closer to him. I tense a little, then relax because, though I don't know him well, there's something about him that makes me trust him. He turns back to the subject I just escaped from. "I know that might've been a little awkward."

I nod.

"But I wish it wasn't," he says, shaking his head. "I'm not sorry for kissing you."

"I don't think I am either," I say. I gaze into his soft blue eyes and bring my lips to his. His lips are parched, dehydrated, screaming for some lip moisturizer, but I don't care. He buries his hand in my hair, holding the back of my head. I let my fingers rest lightly on his broad chest, closing my eyes. I listen to the drumming of Levie's heartbeat against his chest, feeling the pulsing of my own. Then, just when the moment seems perfect, something has to ruin the moment. The thing that ruins this moment is a voice, steady, calling out to someone.

"Levie?" the voice says.

THIRTY-TWO

ASTRI DESMOND IS TALL. She has a heart-shaped face and a hard-set look. She is lean, big, and built with muscles and a tendency to pick fights with others. I recognize her from the party. So she is the girl Levie left to go talk to. She smiled only when she saw Levie. I've come to realize that Astri is not only Levie's friend, but also his bodyguard. His protector. They didn't explicitly say that, but the way she holds a protective stance in front of him, like she's trying to distance him from us, makes me feel like she is more than just a friend. She glares at me with dark eyes hiding under a set of blonde bangs, standing protectively in front of Levie, who just laughs.

"Astri," he says brightly. "Come on." He playfully pushes her to the side, and Astri obliges, but not before flashing him a look of teasing venom.

"So," I say uncomfortably, slipping my hand in Levie's. "Remind me again why you need a bodyguard."

"Oh!" Levie laughs. He laughs too much. "That's because I'm a prince!"

I stop and stare, meeting my eyes to his with disbelief. That's it! That's where I knew his last name. That's why he was so familiar at the party. That's why he just seemed so . . . regal. "Oh, my God!" I don't have anything else to say, I'm so speechless. I fall into a little curtsy.

"Oh, Micah. That is completely unnecessary."

"Oh, my God!" I exclaim with excitement. I've got to stop saying that. Four words echo in my head, and I swell with happiness. I. Kissed. A. Prince. They replay over and over, and I'm trying to make sense of the words running through my head. "Since you're a prince . . ." I say slowly, "do you have transportation?"

"Yeah, I suppose," Levie says. "I have a private hovapod." A hovapod is a pod-shaped aircraft with a rotor on top consisting of three blades. Underneath the pod, four thrusters help stabilize it. The pod is divided into two sections: the first for the pilot and the second for two to six people, depending on the size and model.

"Could you call someone to bring it here?" I ask hopefully. I don't think I can stay in this place anymore. It's too close to Kieling, and it's tainted with bad memories. It might also give us a place to stay for a while as we try to figure out what to do next with the prophecy.

"I guess I could call it," Levie says.

"I forgot Semberic was so old-fashioned with its government!"

Levie grins broadly. "Oh, we're pretty old-fashioned. The people we handle most of the time are aging. Or have aged."

I snort, covering the sharp noise with my hand. "That was a bad joke."

"Aw, seriously?" he says with tease.

I correct myself. "Oh sure. Not bad. Mean." I'm still confused. "Why didn't you tell us before?"

Levie stuffs his hands into his pockets. "I just didn't want it to be weird. I just want to act normal for once. Be a teenager." That makes sense.

"So why are your parents running Semberic in such an old-fashioned way? All the other tribes are run by governments!"

"Definitely not the greatest way to run a tribe," Levie says, scratching the back of his head. "My parents want the world to go back to the 'good old days,' so they're doing what they can to keep the spirit alive. Even for me, their son, it's still unbelievable that they can run a tribe on their own. But my parents get it done. Somehow."

"I'm surprised I didn't notice that you're a prince earlier," I say. "In Divyeine we just focus on training, not learning about the other tribes. I don't agree with Divyeine's terms on not learning about our history, so I do what I can to know about the other tribes." Levie nods. He understands.

"So," I say to change the subject, "you're going to rule as king?"

"Ha! No way. Can't handle that type of work. Once I'm king, I'll convert the system into a modern government."

"But you'll still run it, won't you." It doesn't come out as a question. I know his response.

Levie locks eyes with me. "What are you getting at?" he says, his smile fading, his lips folding over his teeth. I want to talk to him, but with Astri here, discomfort settles in the pit of my stomach. "Can we talk?"

"Of course, Micah." He says it like a proper gentleman. He extends his hand to the side, gesturing for me to move to where his fingers point. "Astri? If you may, will you please give us a moment?"

"Fine, Levie," she says. She moves away, just enough so she's not in earshot of our conversation.

"Are we serious?" I ask Levie.

He looks puzzled for a moment, then answers. "Yes, why?"

"You can't forget about me," I say.

"I'm not," Levie says, shaking his head.

"You're going to be king. You're going to govern a tribe."

Levie laughs. I know it's not intended to hurt me.

"Oh Micah, you must have gotten the wrong idea. I'm not going to be king. I'm not governing the tribe. Someone else is. I can't govern a whole tribe!"

I want to clap my hand against my forehead. "Why?" I say.

"Because . . . I love you."

THIRTY-THREE

"WHO THE HECK IS THIS?" IAN SHOUTS, running across the field to meet us.

Levie and I turn around to face Ian. We haven't uttered a word about what Levie said a few minutes ago. I feel it was too quick to say that. I think we skipped the step of going out on a date and trying things out. I mean, what do I know about love? I could be very wrong about this whole love thing because I have zero experience. The only thing I know about love is from Ian, but he has said he loved me since we were seven, which was some time ago. It makes me think. Is the connection my parents have love? Still, it has literally been two and a half days since Levie and I met, but maybe people in Semberic move quickly through stages that we should be moving through slower because of the purpose of the tribe itself. Maybe all the death jokes have caught up to them.

"Ian," Levie says, "this is Astri."

Astri looks Ian up and down and emits a rather forced smile. "Hey."

"Astri?" Ian says, confused. Then, his face lights up. "I knew it! Levie has a girlfriend."

"Yeah," Levie admits. "Actually, I do." He squeezes my hand lightly.

Ian's eyes twinkle with a rushed shot of happiness. He smiles broadly at me, but his smile vanishes when his vision falls on our hands, clasped together.

"You're not with Astri," Ian says slowly, the sad realization forming in his head.

"I never said I was, Ian," Levie says. Ian frowns and turns on his heel to run back to the cabin, but not before I catch a glimpse of the gleaming tears forming in his eyes.

I shouldn't feel guilty. My life, my relationships. Seeing the tears in his eyes makes me feel conflicted. Is it lingering feelings? I haven't seen him in so long, and I already concluded that I don't have romantic feelings for him anymore, but I am still being hit with negative feelings. I probably shouldn't overthink it. I need to focus on stopping the prophecy from coming true.

THIRTY-FOUR

THE HOVAPOD IS SMALL, fitting a maximum of six people plus the pilot. The pilot regards us with a warm smile, looking at us behind his dark shades. He has a black goatee, and his mop of curly hair is swept under his cap. "Levie, my young prince!" he says. "It's so good to see you, sir."

"Russ!" Levie exclaims, his face glowing. "What has it been? Six years?"

"Yes, indeed. Six years ago I decided to retire, but I kept missing you and your lovely family! I couldn't get over it, so I went looking to see if they kept my spot available."

Russ's eyes fall on Astri.

"Astriana Desmond." Russ nods to her, smile fading.

"Russell," she says curtly.

"Why are you here, Astriana? I didn't know you still served

Levie."

"Why, yes, I do, Russell."

"Please, call me Russ," Russ says through clenched teeth.

"I think I'll call you by your proper name, Russell."

I look back and forth between the two of them. What is going on?

"You know," I say, trying to break up the awkwardness, "why don't I fetch Ian and Fiomi, hmm?"

"That sounds like a great idea, Micah. Thanks," Levie says before kissing my temple.

I'm hoping to forget about the older idiots who say they're the leaders. What do they know? The only thing they can process is how to act like crap. If all of them came together to write a book, the title would most likely be *The Beginner's Guide to Not Working Together and 100 Other Ways to Act Like Idiots.* Unfortunately, they are waiting in the cabin with Ian and Fiomi, so it's hard to ignore the imposters. They aren't imposters really, since the prophecy wasn't clear on who the leaders are—but I'm clear. I am set on being a leader. No one can take my spot. Especially not those kids who are like monkeys gone bananas.

Fiomi is still slumped in the corner. "Hey," I say, rousing her from her glassy-eyed trance.

"What?" she mumbles.

"Come on!" I grab her arm and drag her toward the door. She fights, writhing and slapping my hand repeatedly. I let go.

"Stop it!"

"I'm sorry!" I say. "Please, we have to go." Fiomi closes her eyes, takes a deep breath, and stares at me with crystal clear eyes, ready. When she looks at me, there is no sign that she was ever crying, which is odd.

"Ian," she says, "let's go."

Ian and I exchange glances, and he makes a face, as if to say, are you seeing this? Fiomi bounced back a little too quickly to be normal. Fiomi breezes past Reedecsee, who glares at her.

"Goodbye, Dec. If you would like to, I would be pleased to meet you at Father's." Reedecsee scowls, but nods.

"What do you mean?" I ask Fiomi.

"I think I'm going to stay with my father for a while. Just to calm down. I'll join you later, Micah. Is that all right?"

"B-but what about the prophecy?" I sputter.

She turns away with a wave of her hand. "You don't need me. You have Levie and Ian. I need time to be alone. I'll also notify my parents of Natalia's death, since where we were is still Kieling land."

"We can't do this without you!" I panic. There's a stone, building itself up in my stomach, then falling, falling. Hitting the bottom. I wince.

"You okay?" Ian says.

I don't mean to be dramatic. I don't. So I say: "Yeah. Of course. We have to go. Levie and Astri are waiting."

"Okay."

THIRTY-FIVE

"SO YOU'RE JUST GOING TO LEAVE US?" Farrah says, running to keep up with our long strides. In her hand, she holds clean white sneakers.

"Um, it's not like we were planning on taking five extra people in the first place."

"It's fine," she says. "The five of us will go to Semberic on foot. It won't take long."

"It won't take long?" I laugh cruelly, though I don't intend for it to be. "You're passing through all of Kieling. That will take days, weeks! Auneaire isn't as small as it seems to be on maps."

"Yeah, I know. If it were that small, then you and I would be best friends," Farrah says, leaning down so her dress hangs loose around her slim body. Fair point. She slips on the pair of sneakers on her bare tan feet. "But like I told you: it's fine."

I shrug. "Fine, but by the time you get there we'll probably be gone. We have a world to save. Staying in one tribe for weeks doesn't help us complete our tasks."

Farrah raises her eyebrows and brushes her long hair, which is swept in a ponytail, over her shoulder. "You heard about the prophecy?"

"Of course." I say it like it's obvious.

"So you know that we're the leaders?"

"No. Last time I checked, we were."

"Oh God, please. Take my spot. I didn't want to do this. Foster did. I only follow like the good sister I am."

"Please," I drawl, "save me from boredom. I don't have a brother, and I'm really glad I don't." Though I have a poker face, on the inside I'm dancing with joy, knowing that I convinced Farrah and Denzel that they don't have to continue with the prophecy. Hopefully now they will drop out of being leaders.

"You don't wish to have a buddy?"

"I don't need one. I have Ian. If I had a brother, he would only get in my way." My voice lowers. "I don't think I would be able to bear watching anyone getting hurt. I already heard myself getting beat up."

Farrah cocks her head. "What?"

"Never mind," I say, waving my hand away, ending the conversation about my abusive parents. There's a sort of relief to not talking about that. It's like opening the cage of a bird I know will never return, not after it got hurt. Its wing healed, so it flew away. It was hurt, and it didn't want to go back to where fate had almost trapped it. The bird flew away.

THIRTY-SIX

LEVIE SMILES, trying to break up the awkwardness between Astri and Russell. Astri climbs into the hovapod without asking for permission, hooking her fingers around a handle and hauling herself up into the aircraft. Farrah and I are close enough to the hovapod to be in earshot of what Levie and Astri are saying.

Levie leans on the side of the hovapod. "Astriana," he muses, letting the new word slide. "I didn't know your name was Astriana," he admits.

Astri scowls. "There's a lot of things you don't know about me. First thing—I go by Astri. I don't care if my parents named me Astriana."

Levie tilts his head and squints at her. If she wants to play that way, he'll play along. "All right," he says, grinning. Testing her. "Second thing I should probably know: what's going on between you two? I've never seen Russell act like that before, and now you dare talk to me like I'm not a prince."

Astri sniggers. "You may be a prince," she says, her voice lowering. "You may be the person whom I'm assigned to protect, but you are my friend. I view the two of us as equal, no one bigger or smaller than the other. Got it?"

"Got it," Levie agrees. I wonder if he thinks of the kiss. He seemed surprised when I made the move, but he seemed glad that it happened because he kissed me back. I wonder if he thinks I had guts. He seems like the type of person who's had experience, so maybe this was newer. Maybe my nerve was why he told me he loved me so soon.

THIRTY-SEVEN

I WALK TO THE HOVAPOD, Ian striding next to me. Levie smiles.

"Where's Fiomi?" he asks. I shake my head. Levie's smile fades. "She's not coming?"

"No," Ian responds.

Levie's face darkens, and he hops into the hovapod. "Let's go."

I sit next to Levie, and we strap in. Ian peeps a little hello to Russ, who acknowledges him with a nod. Ian plops down next to Astri, and pulls the seatbelt over himself, pushing it so it clicks. He doesn't look on me. He's probably still hurt from earlier, though his stoic face doesn't give anything away. I'll give him time; our announcement was a lot to take in.

The hovapod starts to rumble, running over the grass. I take out a pocketknife and slice open my fish, removing any bones I can find. I don't really have anything proper to put it on, but Levie hands me a handkerchief from the breast pocket of his button-down. Piece by piece, I chew on the fish thoughtfully. It tastes so good. It has a smoky taste, and it is still warm from the remains of the fire. I offer some to Levie, who just shakes his head. The hovapod tilts and lifts off the ground. I press my hands to the window, staring out of it. I can see the small dark figures of Farrah and her friends, and Fiomi, waving wildly from below. Fiomi flashes me one last grin before we rise too far for her to be seen.

THIRTY-EIGHT

ASTRI SITS, her spine straight, her body rigid. It seems as though she has frozen over, and the things that give her away are little things: how she blinks every now and then, the subtle rise and fall of her chest, the way she parts her lips ever so slightly to exhale. She regards me with a toxic look, squinting at my fingers interlaced with Levie's, as if to shield her eyes from the blinding sun. I feel the bumpiness of the air that surrounds us. I lean back and feel the cool metal of the jet's side press against my back. A sharp jerk, and the hovapod veers to the left, caught off guard by the blast of wind that rattles its metal and glass structure. The hovapod shakes. I feel ready for my thin body to topple out of the seat, since I'm not secured by the seat belt. The thrusters underneath help with stability during turbulence, so the ride would be much, much worse without them. The wind howls and screams, racing through every open hole and crevice it can penetrate, squeezing and shoving. Levie clenches my hand hard, his head thrown back, his mouth bursting with air. His eyes are squeezed shut, and he peeps a moan.

"I don't feel so good," he wails quietly to me. His whole body is flattened to the side of the hovapod, the skin on his face turning a sickly shade of green.

"Just breathe," I say calmly. I don't get motion sickness. He attempts to turn to look at me, he tries, and he fails. He pushes against the wall, groaning, sliding his hands down his face.

"I've flown so many times, but I never get used to it. I keep doing it, over and over, but I don't think that this is ever going to go away."

I reach into my backpack and offer Levie a stick of gum. "Do you think I can eat right now?" he asks.

"C'mon," I say. "It helps." Levie accepts my offer and chews the gum, resting his head on the metal side of the plane.

Levie still isn't well enough to say anything, but he nods a little in thanks.

I lean forward, so my arms rest on my knees. "Astri," I say.

"What?" she scowls.

"What was up with you and Russ?" Russ is close enough to

hear, but he doesn't say anything. He just focuses on guiding the plane safely through the clouds.

To my surprise, she answers. "We just had a fight. That's all."

Levie stifles a laugh. "Why would you guys have a fight? You barely interact."

Astri looks at her hands and says, "I'm just not exactly like-able."

THIRTY-NINE

BY THE TIME WE GET TO SEMBERIC, the sun has set, and the moon takes over. I've never been to Semberic before. It's a quiet tribe. I also notice that Levie didn't lie. An enormous palace sits in the middle of the whole tribe, the building taking up around one-sixth of the whole tribe itself. It's that big. Russ guides the hova-pod to land safely on the runway, rolling until it comes to a stop before the palace. I get out and gape at the giant building. Ian grins, and his eyes twinkle. Levie spreads his hands out in front of him. I survey the palace, which is empty, except for the few guards standing in front of the huge doors. Lampposts are erected along the walkways, shining down on us.

"Come inside," Levie says. He leads like a prince should: his hands clasped behind his back, his posture straight, his eyes focused ahead. He has his nose in the air in a manner that is not arrogant, but proud. Just enough.

The guards push open the doors, revealing the grand hallway. The hallway is lined with paintings and armor stands carrying tarnished silver armor. The paintings are of each member of the Tanelo family: one for the mother of the king, the king, the queen, and Levie. I stare in awe at Levie's painting—its swirls and textures, blends of colors to perfect Levie's skin tone and eyes. I reach out to touch Painting Levie's lips, cheeks, hair. Feel the roughness of the paint against my fingertips. Below, a gold plate with the words Levian Carell Tanelo inscribed into it is tacked on the wall. I touch that, too, and feel the cool of the metal. Of course, Levie would prefer to have a name that doesn't sound as elegant as his full name.

"Let's go, Micah," Ian says, grinning. I link my arm through his because, while we used to hold hands all the time, it's too intimate for the circumstances. We follow Levie, Astri at his side. Levie explains that his parents are in the throne room, which is to the left of us, but he takes us up a staircase instead.

"Where are we going?" I ask. "I want to meet your parents!"

"I'm going to show you your rooms," Levie says, eyes twinkling. "It's been a long day, don't you think?"

I look out a window once we reach the landing. It is very dark now. The stars glitter. I remember a poem my mother told me once. I remember it vaguely, for when she told me that poem, I was little, and she was not yet abusive. The stars remind me of the poem. *There's a place farther than the naked eye can see. It's so beautiful and so perfect that no one can believe it. But it's there, we know it, the silver light gleams. Though you must get to it before the stars start to bleed.* The poem means a lot to me. It means my parents shared something so beautiful with me. Yes, my parents did that. I don't remember it wrong.

FORTY

LEVIE SHOWS US TO OUR ROOMS, each on the same floor as his. Ian's room is right across from mine, and Levie's is at the end of the hall. I walk into mine slowly and take in what I'm seeing. I've never been in such a gorgeous room before. It must be at least twenty-five feet by twenty-five feet. It's so large, so beautiful, so unlike the room I have at my house. The bedding is made of silk, the pillows too, both colored a soft peach. The carpet is a creme color. A vanity table stands in one corner of the room, a dresser at another. The ceiling has a skylight, as well as a crystal chandelier that hangs down in glittering strands. There is a closet lined with gold.

I drop my backpack, shut the door, and sink into the bed. It feels so gentle to the touch, so smooth and soft. I want to crawl under the covers, but I'm not tired yet. I change into much more comfortable clothes—a pair of gray silk sweatpants and a matching tank top. Once I'm ready, with my feet pushed into plush slippers, I creep out and head to Levie's room. This place is so grand.

Levie's room is surprisingly smaller than mine. It's carpeted in light blue, with a midnight blue canopy bed taking up the center. It's also noticeably less extravagant than mine. Sure, the things in it look like they are from a palace, but Levie's room doesn't have a brilliant chandelier or anything like that. The bedsheets and pillow are still made of silk, but everything's so simple. I don't see Levie, so I just explore his room. On top of his dresser, he has rubber dinosaurs and a few textbooks. I'm surprised I didn't know that Levie is a prince. I feel like I should have known, but I've been so caught up with everything else in my life that I just forgot, I suppose. Posters of Larveson bands are plastered on one wall. Glow-in-the-dark stars are pressed on the ceiling. I walk around a little more and find a bathroom.

The bathroom floor has diamond-shaped tiles and a marble countertop with a toothbrush, toothpaste, a water cup, and a container full of a green liquid that looks like mouthwash. I face a mirror. There's a toilet, bathtub, and a shower, all of which are high-tech. I scoot out of the bathroom and into his walk-in closet, which is about the size of my room at home. It's lined with shelves, all of which are carrying stacks of shirts, pants, undergarments, swimwear. The bottom row holds pairs of shoes for all different occasions. On hooks he hangs his formal wear such as blazers, button-downs, tuxedos, and a lot of other clothes I can't name because I've never seen them before. He also hangs his jackets there. Levie stands in the middle, his back facing me. His back is bare, his legs covered by plaid pajama pants. He probably doesn't know I'm here. He runs his pointer finger across the shelves and stops at a plain red T-shirt. He lifts the stack of shirts off it carefully, slides the shirt out, and replaces the shirts neatly. I clear my throat.

"Hi," I say.

Levie jumps around. "What are you doing here?" he asks, startled, dropping his red shirt. I shrug. I fight off the urge to smile first because Levie's just so beautiful, and I can't help myself.

"Just wanted to explore."

Levie examines my clothes. He smiles. "That looks good on you."

I give him a smile of my own. "Yeah?"

"Yeah," he says, reaching out to place his hands on my shoulders, bringing me closer. We stand there, just like that, in a tentative embrace but with a feeling of safety surrounding us.

FORTY-ONE

THE ROOFTOP GARDEN IS A SMALL YET A GLORIOUS SIGHT. I emerge from the doorway and view it with amazement. It is so very beautiful. It consists of a white gazebo, with ivy and other vines twisting themselves around its wooden beams. There are a few flower beds, the flowers arranged so they sit in rainbow order. I remember when I saw the Cate family's grass. This is so much better. Everything in Divyeine is bland, nothing special about it. No flowers, or dirt, just the bare necessities to survive. Inside the gazebo, there is a dainty coffee table and a bench, where Ian sits. I did not expect Ian to be here. But he's here anyway.

I sit next to Ian and lean into him. I haven't really leaned against my best friend like this in a long time, and it pains me that I don't feel as comfortable doing so as I used to. His eyes have lost what they used to have. They aren't full anymore. He's like a glass of water not yet full. It was, once, but someone poured out some of the water. I know what he's missing. I can sense his longing, his want. He's chasing something, reaching for it, but it moves farther away, farther up the road. He can't keep up, so he just stops.

His touch doesn't feel the same. Even though he still holds his arms around me like he used to, even though I still breathe in the same scent, still feel his touch, it feels like he's not here at all. Ian feels like a ghost.

His eyes glint with moonlight, and he gives me a tight smile, but it doesn't reach his eyes. He's changed. "I'm sorry," he says, his voice cracking slightly. I hope he doesn't feel my heart break inside me, the pieces dropping to the bottom.

I shake my head, squeeze my eyes shut. I wrap my arms around him and hold him tight, opening my eyes every few seconds to make sure he's still here with me. This whole time I've been so focused on Levie that I haven't thought much about Ian. Sure, a thought or two wandered into my mind sometimes, but the thoughts about Levie are too selfish to make room for anything else. I want to tell Ian that I still love him. I do. I care for him. He's my best friend. But I don't say anything, I keep silent. He knows already. He just chooses not to believe it.

We aren't as close as we once were, and that's a fact. We're still best friends, but just barely. To tell the truth, right now the person who knows the most about me, and the person who I thought I knew the most about as well, is like a stranger. I don't know who he is anymore. There are just so many unanswered questions about him that I can't answer myself. I don't know what thoughts are running through his head, even though I used to be able to tell what he was feeling. But he's not the only one who's changed. I've changed, too. I look different, I feel different, about things. Yes, he was my light, but right now, I don't think it's bright enough to light the way.

It feels selfish of me. Having a friend here who stuck with me through thick and thin should make me feel better, not guilty. It's probably because I've sort of been avoiding him since we reunited. I began thinking about other things and stopped thinking about Ian. Deep down, he's one of the most important people in my life, but I haven't been showing it, so maybe that's why I feel guilty. Because part of this is my fault. My stomach twists and a lump forms in my throat, but I don't cry.

I don't watch the tears roll down his face. He rests his chin on my head, closes his eyes. I don't need to see him cry. He never cries. He never cries when I'm around. I close my eyes because I don't need to see the tears I know are there.

Ian, I think. *I'm sorry too.* We're both sorry to each other. And for me at least, I'm sorry that what we had is just not enough anymore.

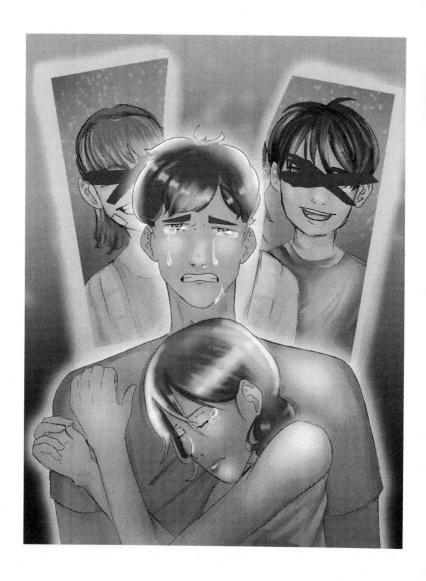

FORTY-TWO

I DON'T SEE IAN OVER THE NEXT FEW DAYS. It might be because the palace is so big. But usually, we roam in a group. Or at least, Levie and I walk around together. The other reason is because he needed to get away. Like I needed to. Maybe to mourn Natalia's death. Maybe to think. Maybe both. Maybe just to heal a broken heart.

So, I use this time to think. How was Natalia murdered right under our noses? Who could it be? Could it be Reedecsee? I know she was angry with Fiomi. Fiomi probably brought Natalia into the house before. They were close friends. Reedecsee might've seen them together and thought Natalia could be used as collateral damage, but it went the wrong way. No, that doesn't make sense. The prophecy is being followed. One of the leaders has died. The creator of the prophecy has to be smart, meticulous, organized. This person has to map out every move, do everything just right. No way could a disorganized and dumb person create a prophecy.

Right. The prophecy. I need to write this down. I look in a file cabinet and find a stack of paper. I pull out a pen and then take out the crumped newspaper from my backpack. Then, I seat myself at the vanity table and start scribbling on a piece of paper:

Who has access to the Divyeine newspaper?

- News reporters

- Government officials

- Anonymous people

Okay, wait. Anonymous people. They're allowed to put some stuff in the newspaper. The editors look through the submissions. No way would they allow some prophecy written by someone anonymous to take up a page. Usually those submissions are just little boxes. So this has to be someone with some sort of authority. Someone with control. I do know one person who was acting odd with Natalia's death: Fiomi. She's the daughter of the man who governs Kieling. That gives her some sort of authority. She might also have the authority to contact someone from Divyeine to do her dirty work. I've never heard of any violence happening with people from tribes other than Divyeine. When Fiomi looked up at me when we were about to leave, her eyes were dry. I would have been crying for hours. That gets me thinking. I can't find Ian, and Fiomi isn't under our watch.

She could be doing a lot, now that she separated from the people who are trying to stop this massacre. She could be planning something. And now that Ian isn't here, he could be in danger.

Then a thought hits me—another leader hasn't died yet that we know of, but I think Ian might be the next victim.

FORTY-THREE

I STILL HAVEN'T SEEN IAN, and I'm starting to worry. If Ian went somewhere outside the palace, he could be in a lot of danger if Fiomi somehow finds him. If Fiomi really is the person who killed Natalia, she could be extra dangerous. It makes me sick to think that it could be her. What would she want so badly that she would kill her best friend to get it? I've had no contact with Fiomi; I'm unable to reach her. She isn't answering her phone. I try not to think of what might have happened to Ian. I don't want to get out of bed, but I do. I have to. There's nothing I can do. I drag myself to get dressed. Then, I push myself to the bathroom to brush my hair, which is so messed up from the night of turning and tossing that it sticks up in a very unflattering way.

Levie waits for me outside my door, and arm in arm we walk down the staircase. We walk through the grand hallway, past

Levie's portrait, and into a room I haven't explored yet. The ceiling is tall and adorned with gold and swirls of paint. In the center of the room, near the far wall, stand two thrones. On them sit two people. It's the grandest room in this palace that I've ever been in. I've been hidden for a week, yet Mr. and Mrs. Tanelo act as though they haven't noticed me at all, which I doubt.

Today I am going to officially meet Levie's parents. I suck in a deep breath and find myself face to face with Mr. and Mrs. Tanelo.

The two are aging; wrinkles are etched into their facial features. Both carry salt-and-pepper hair. The king's hair is slicked back. He sports a short beard and a dark suit. He is tall and lean. The queen has her hair pulled back in a bun. She is wearing a gray gown that flows to the floor. The gown has small gems sewn into the neckline and the ends of the sleeves. I can see that Levie gets his eyes from his mother. Her eyes are blue like the ocean. His are, too.

A wave of emotion washes over the king's and queen's faces, but I cannot decipher which. Maybe excitement. They don't look angry, so I relax.

"Levian," the king says politely, though his calm mask ripples with delight.

"Father."

"You look good this morning, son."

"Thank you, Father."

Levie wears a white button-down shirt and black pants. His shirt tucks into his pants. It has no wrinkles, just sharp creases where they should be.

"Levian." The queen speaks now. "Would you be kind enough to introduce this young, gorgeous lady?" She smiles at me warmly.

"Mother," Levie says, "This is Micah Bourrow."

"Micah Bourrow," the king says thoughtfully. "I've never heard of the name. Tell me, my dear, how come I haven't seen you around?"

"Father," Levie says, his tone airy. "Micah is from Divyeine."

I half expect Mr. and Mrs. Tanelo to recoil in fear or maybe kick me out of their house like everyone else did or hand me to the law, but they just smile. "Thank you," the king says. "Thank you for protecting us."

I smile at them. "Thank you, sir. I appreciate it. But actually, I haven't fought in any war."

"You'll get there, then?"

"Actually, sir," I say, "I'm not sure I really want to risk my life. It's just not … me."

The queen places a hand on my shoulder. Her forehead creases, marked with permanent wrinkles. "I understand, dear. Life is full of surprises—you are one of them." I can't decide whether that was meant to be a compliment or not. I just thank her. Nod, smile, thank. That's how a royal should act. I do decide that I enjoy being treated as a royal. Living in this lavish lifestyle. I may enjoy it, but that doesn't mean I belong here.

FORTY-FOUR

I LOOK AT MY CLOCK. It's just after eight o'clock, and the sun has finally set. It stretched over the horizon and then just sank. Someone knocks at my door. It must be Levie; we planned to sit in the gazebo together tonight. I smooth down my red dress, unlock the door, and smile at the face who greets me. But it's not who I expect.

Ian stands in front of me, his hands stuffed in his pockets, his expression serene. My first instinct is to pull him into a hug and breathe in his vanilla almond smell and hug him and hug—

I pull my arm back and slap him on the face. Red spreads from his cheek, across his nose, to his other cheek.

He sighs. "I deserve that," he says. "I'm sorry."

"You better be sorry!" I cry, pulling him into my room and rushing to embrace him. I squeeze him tight. "Where have you been?" I say, so softly it's almost under my breath.

"I just needed to think."

"About?"

"Everything, Micah. First, I had to mourn Natalia's death. I had to think about what you said. And when I'm coming back Fiomi dies and—"

"What?"

FORTY-FIVE

EVERYTHING HAS STOPPED—TIME AND ME. I can't move. I'm caught between the acts of slumping to the floor or crying or holding my head in my hands. I do all of the above. My mouth is suddenly dry, and my stomach curdles like bad milk.

I click on the television in my room and watch in horror as the news reporter shows a disturbing video of the large Kieling house bursting into flames. Everything repeats itself in slow motion.

All my suspicions come crumbling down. I finally had a lead, but this changes everything.

I can't shake the vision of the house exploding. The fire eating up the magnificent cloth and wood and glass and metal. Everything just gone. The camera zooms in on a blue carcass of something: the velvety blue armchair where Zesten had sat. Then the camera twists, and I see debris and smoke and fire and concrete reduced to a cinder, to rubble. The camera zooms in on another something. Something that draws my attention. Something that makes me feel so sick to my stomach that I double over and Ian has to catch me, saving me from a fall. The camera zooms in on a pair of brown and black glasses.

FORTY-SIX

I CLUTCH MY STOMACH, retching. Vomit rolls off my tongue and lands on the carpet at my feet. Two of my friends dead. Gone. Poof. Just like that. They're not coming back.

My knees buckle, and I clench my stomach, my cheeks streaked with fat tears. I lower my head to my chest and just sob. I sob so hideously. There are too many people to be lost because of this prophecy.

There's only one person who could die out of the three of us who remain. I'm not scared to die. Everyone who has died was murdered. It wasn't by accident. Someone killed them on purpose. That's what I'm scared of. I'm scared to see who is killing these people. I'm scared that I'm the next victim, given to them without a choice. I said I wasn't scared of dying. Being murdered is a different story.

FORTY-SEVEN

LEVIE KNOWS ABOUT WHAT HAPPENED. I can tell from the grim look on his face. It's night now. I'm glad for it. I like the dark because it hides me. It hides my tears. Ian has locked himself in his room.

At first, I was tempted to yell at Ian and ask him where he had been, but now I find that irrelevant and foolish. I'm now angry and grieving over Fiomi's sudden and unexpected death.

I can hear conversation from the television streaming downstairs, sounding not grim, but neutral. It is on high volume, blasting so loud it reaches my ears. I can hear the words loud and clear.

"The attack on Kieling's leader Zesten Bianco was unexpected. Unfortunately, Mr. Bianco and his fourteen-year-old daughter Fiomi Bianco did not escape the building before it collapsed. Authorities have identified Mr. Bianco's stepdaughter Reedecsee Garmond as deceased as well. Authorities have suspects, but they have announced they are not holding anyone liable for the bombing of the Kieling government building, at the moment."

Reedecsee? She's dead too? Before, Fiomi and Reedecsee were so hostile to each other, but I suppose they got together to try to patch things up. Reedecsee wasn't exactly pleasant when we met, but the thought of yet another death haunts me. Even though I grew up in the tribe where most deaths occur, Natalia's death was the first time I had ever truly seen what a corpse, and what death, looks like.

I understand why the news reporter says authorities are not holding anyone liable. The authorities are Divyeine. I know Divyeine. They won't admit that they did it. But everyone knows they did. No other tribe has the materials or technology to pull off an attack like that.

FORTY-EIGHT

I FIND LEVIE SITTING ON THE EDGE OF HIS BED, his fingers curled tightly around his sheets. I sit next to him, and he wraps his arms around me. I pull in a shaky breath.

"You're serious about the prophecy, right?" I ask.

"Of course," he says. "I mean, I was sort of just pulled into it, but I'm serious about it, yes."

"So you know that you can die, and yet you're still in it," I say, my face shadowed with trepidation and sadness.

"I don't care if I die." Levie laughs sharply. "I'm here with you, and right now you are all that matters."

My stomach flutters. "I love you," I say.

"I love you," he responds. Then he pulls me in for a kiss, and as I feel our lips meet, warmth flows through me, and I flush deeply. I feel so lucky to have someone like him.

I think about what would happen if I told Ian that I loved him, those eight years ago. We would have still found each other. We would have met by the Willow, and Ian's small hands would close around my own, and we'd be so happy. We'd be so happy. Look at him now. I force myself to stop thinking about Ian because he is not the one I want, and the one I want is sitting right in front of me, lips met to mine.

FORTY-NINE

LEVIE. I need to get to Levie. There is no doubt that he is next. I said it could be anyone out of the three of us. But the terrible part of it is that I believe Ian. When he said we'd be fine. I feel sick because I believe him and know he's right. Who wouldn't want to murder a prince? I wouldn't. That's why I need to find him.

He's not in his room. That's when I start to panic. Because Levie's almost always in his room.

My dried tears are frozen on my face, and I suddenly turn cold. Where is he? I haven't seen Ian either. And he just got back.

I hurry to the rooftop garden hoping that Levie is there, but I don't see him. So I head downstairs to ask the king and queen, but they just shrug and tell me to check in the pool area, which I haven't been to yet. They send me off with simple instructions, and I find my way there.

The pool is lined with turquoise tile, and so is the jacuzzi. The jacuzzi bubbles pop and sizzle. Thick steam rises into the air. Thick, red steam. The water in the jacuzzi is cherry red from blood spilling out of a body lying face up in the hot foam. Blond hair, dripping with teardrops of water, flows from the scalp of the head. The body is half-naked, only covered by swim shorts. The body's feet are bare and bloodless. The slit is long, but not wide. It was most likely made by the tip of a blade, for the width of the cut probably measures two millimeters or so, but even so, the wound is deep. It snakes its way from the right collarbone, crossing diagonally to the chest area, near the heart. It goes deeper there. Then, it trails down to the stomach, which also has a slit made by a knife, possibly the same. That knife wound punctured the vital organs, and the damage was immensely severe. That is what caused the real damage, besides the blood that was profusely bleeding and not stifled.

Instantly, I swear and swish away some of the bubbles, only to drop down in disbelief at the lifeless body floating in the water.

No. I had the knotted feeling in my gut, but I refused to believe it, and I still do. I stayed in Levie's room last night. I slept in his bed, and he took the floor. I insisted that he could sleep in the bed, and I could take the floor, but he turned down the demurral and insisted. He got up in the morning, shook me awake ever so slightly to let me know where he was going, kissed me on the head, and left, towel in hand. He told me he was going to the gym. I was too exhausted to notice that Levie was wearing swim shorts. And now here he floats, bare, cold, and dead.

FIFTY

I PULL LEVIE UP WITH MY REMAINING STRENGTH. My muscles burn because most of my strength was drained once I saw him. Too much has happened, and it has all happened so quickly.

I lean down and press my lips to Levie's for one last kiss before he is whisked away, but as I do, I immediately withdraw. His lips are cold, and I know that he's dead, but it feels almost fake and unreal. He's lifeless, and he's not reaching up to trace my jawline or to tangle his fingers in my hair. He's not going to look at me with those beautiful eyes he had, and he's never going to smile the smile that made me fall so deeply in love with him. He's never going to turn his head back to face me with a loving glance, and he won't whisper I love you to me anymore. He won't smell like his usual citrusy scent that comes from his soap. He's never going to say anything again.

This hits me all at once, like a blow to my stomach. I drape myself over his still-bleeding body and cry. I scream hard, but no sound comes out. Like I have no voice. Like I had given him my voice and he took it but tossed it away because he knew he couldn't use it. There's no use in screaming if there's no sound. I'll lose my voice no matter what comes from my lips. The sound is just from the shrill wailing of sirens.

I expect the king and queen to get angry at me, for them to kick me out like everyone else has, but they embrace me like they're my own parents. I cry in the arms of the queen, who holds me tightly as if I'm a baby, but I need the hug, and I accept it.

"I love him," I whisper through tears. He loved me, and I still love him.

"I know, dear, I know. I love him too." Then, we're all quiet for a moment, listening to my sniffling and to the sirens warbling in the background.

FIFTY-ONE

THINGS ARE DIFFERENT NOW THAT LEVIE'S DEAD. It's been four weeks, and Ian and I have continued fighting with one another. Astri was fired because she wasn't able to protect Levie. Boo her.

Levie's funeral was long ago already, though I lost track of exactly how long ago it was. It was a small gathering, even though he was a prince. It was just the king and queen, Ian, Russ, Astri, her parents, and me. It was held on the rooftop garden.

Levie has a small gravestone though he was cremated, something he asked of his parents long before he was murdered. The gravestone is placed upright in one of the flowerbeds, the one carrying the violets and the dahlias. Every time I walk past that flowerbed, it feels like someone has punched me in the gut, and I try to shrug it off, but the image of Levie with his bare torso flashes in my mind, the red slits stretching themselves across his chest

and his stomach. I shudder and force back the tears that are starting to well up. These past few weeks I haven't gotten good sleep.
Nightmares are forcing themselves into my mind, and I feel sick
from them.

I think back to the nightmare I had last night:

I walk along the rooftop garden, breathing in the sweet aroma
of the flowers. I run my fingers along the surface of the fence en-
closing part of the gazebo, walking all the way around until I
come to the entrance. Levie emerges from the doorway leading
to the hall, his chest bare as well as his feet. He wears a pair of
swim shorts and a steady grin. He walks toward me slowly and
breathes an "I love you" in my hair. I put my hands on his chest and
smile at him, and we lean in closer to kiss, but my right hand feels
encased in something wet, warm, and sticky. Then my hand starts
to sink in that something. I look down, shocked, to see a deep red
slit opening wide and eating away at Levie's flesh. I attempt to
shut my eyes from the horrific and gruesome sight, but I'm unable
to, so I'm forced to watch Levie's lips get sucked away by the invisible entity that challenged him to a duel and won. Levie's face
practically melts into nothingness, and what's left collapses into
a pile of bones, blood, and battered brains.

That's when my dream wakes me up. I wish I had control over

my dreams so I could stop myself from watching such a disgusting sight. But I can only wish, and like I've said before, I've learned that wishes don't come true.

FIFTY-TWO

WHEN I GET BACK INTO MY ROOM IN THE PALACE, I take out that piece of paper again. I look so angrily at it. I crumple it and throw it across the room. Then I scream. I can't help it. I hadn't lost anybody I really truly loved, and now I have. It hurts so much. Then, I pick the paper back up, smooth it out, and glare at it. I dive into thinking about the mystery so I don't have to think about Levie as much, so it'll hurt less. Ian and I are the only leaders still alive. I thought Fiomi murdered Natalia. She's smart; she's from Kieling. But just because someone isn't from Kieling doesn't mean they aren't smart. And yes, I know Fiomi was suspicious, but she could have really been crying. And I'm going to be honest, I barely knew her. Or Natalia. Or even Levie, but Levie and I had an immediate connection, so I trusted him. Ian and I are the only ones left. Ian left before Fiomi died. Why did Ian leave? I don't think it was to mend a broken heart. I think he was plotting. He was planning. He wasn't here when Fiomi died, and when he was here, Levie died. It has to be him.

I don't want to believe it. No, I can't jump to conclusions so quickly, not like I did with Fiomi. It wouldn't make sense for Ian to kill anyone either. For as long as I have known him, to me, he has been the sweet boy I always knew. I don't want to accept it, but I think subconsciously, I need someone to blame.

I receive a ping on my phone, so I pick it up from my vanity table. There is a text from Ian: *Can we meet for lunch in downtown Semberic? I want to talk.* Ian then sends me details about the venue and the time I should meet him. It's scary to think about meeting with him, but I don't have any concrete evidence that he is the killer, so I just breathe and text him back, saying that I'll meet him soon.

I meet him around twelve-thirty at a small restaurant in the heart of the tribe. During the day, the city is surprisingly a very lively place—full of music, dancing, and happy people. Children frolic in the streets while adults chat quietly, all carrying smiles on their faces. For a tribe with a dark purpose, it is a tribe that is so alive. It's not like that in Divyeine.

Though, I suppose I can't really compare that to Divyeine.

These people are allowed to go to each other's tribes, to learn, to help each other, whatever. They're allowed to interact, so it shouldn't surprise me that this is a very lively place. The people who are here aren't just from Semberic. As for Divyeine, we're isolated because we can't get distracted from other things. Fighting and enforcing the law is our sole purpose in life.

The restaurant is quaint, clean, and organized. The outside of the restaurant is a shocking pink, which I suppose draws attention to this apparently well-known place. People sit outside, eating and talking. I immediately love it as soon as I walk in. Smells of tea and sweets reach my nose, and I eagerly breathe them in. In one corner stands a counter with a cashier. Behind it are shiny white coffee mugs, a tray full of fresh-baked sundaiberry scones, and a smoothie machine. Sundaiberries are large round berries, about the size of small plums, that vary in color, usually in shades of yellow or orange. Their skin is edible, smooth, and thin. They grow in sunny regions, hence the name sundaiberry. They live in hot regions like the Pembermane Desert. The Pembermane Desert is a building with the inside built to resemble a desert. Technology inside the building makes the climate suit whatever grows inside, such as the sundaiberries. The seemingly open, natural environments in Auneaire are about as real as movie sets. The plants are real, the sand and water are real, but they're all land-scaped. I've come to know that everything in Auneaire isn't really real. Even friendships.

Personally, I adore sundaiberries, but I'm not different from others when it comes to the fruit. Because the environment of Auneaire isn't natural, the farmers who grow the sundaiberries make sure that each one grows perfectly sweet and round.

Ian is sitting at a table near the window, staring out blankly, cupping a mug of tea. He has an untouched scone on his plate. I hang my worn backpack on the corner of my chair and force a smile at him.

"Hey," I say.

"Hey!" Ian says as he gets up and hugs me. I flinch, but he doesn't notice. He goes back to his seat, and I settle in mine. He signals for a waitress and asks for another sundaiberry scone. The waitress smiles as she returns to set it on the table. Ian pushes the triangle-shaped sweet to me. I take it gladly and bite into it, tasting the sweetness of the sundaiberry as well as the subtle sweetness of the scone.

"So, you wanted to talk?" I ask. It's almost a rhetorical question, but I ask it just to keep Ian going.

"Yes," Ian says. "I wanted to talk to you about the prophecy."

I tense. "What about it?"

"We are the remaining two. You know we have to get the moonstone." He bites into his scone, drops it from his hand, and stands up abruptly. "Excuse me," he chokes out before making a run for the restroom. The waitress gives me a concerned expression, and I make my move.

FIFTY-THREE

I DON'T STOP TO THINK THAT ANOTHER MALE MIGHT BE USING THE RESTROOM. My only thought is Ian. I kick the door open and stop to hear retching from the stall nearest me. I walk to the open stall and hover over him. Ian must have been in such a hurry he didn't bother to lock the door. "Ian?" I say with genuine worry in my voice.

He turns his head a little. "What the hell, Micah? Why are you in here?"

"I had to check on you. Are you okay? What happened?"

"It's just my dysphagia. I wanted to eat that damn scone. I thought I might be okay. I just wanted to be normal." He slumps against the bathroom stall and rests his head on the wall.

I sink down and hold his head to my chest, wondering what to do. I shouldn't be doing anything except comforting him. He seems so broken right now, almost convincing me that he isn't the killer, but I'm still wary, and I cannot let my guard down.

***

Once Ian has calmed down, I tell him, "We need to go to Divyeine."

"Yes," Ian agrees. "But I think you should not come."

My brow furrows. "What do you mean?"

"Because if your mother sees you again, you will be in a vulnerable position. You don't have control over her."

"I'm not going anywhere near my mother! You know my house isn't close to the government building."

Ian sighs. "I just don't want you getting hurt."

I ignore my guilt and turn on him angrily. "I understand that, Ian. I've lived in Divyeine all my life. I know what Divyeine is like. I've been hurt before. They're all like my parents. Yet you act as if you know more than me!" I hiss.

"What has gotten into you?" Ian says. His face hardens.

"You don't know me, so stop pretending like you do!" My voice starts to rise.

"I know you! We told each other everything!"

"Years ago! Stop acting like you know me, Ian. It's been eight years since then." I glare at him.

"Fine," he says bitterly. "Maybe I was just acting this way because I was trying to hold onto the memory of something I wouldn't accept is gone! You're not the Micah I remember."

I smirk and aggressively stand up from the floor. I pivot on my heel, but before I walk out of the stall, I look back at him, staring into his hazel-green eyes.

"And you're not the Ian I remember, either." I start walking, then stop again. I seethe silently. "The Ian you are now is much, much worse." And with that, I leap out of the stall and storm out of the restaurant, letting Ian pay for my half-eaten sundaiberry scone.

FIFTY-FOUR

FOR COUNTLESS DAYS, I stay holed up in my bedroom. I just watch the clock on my wall, ticking every second.

Tick.

Tock.

Tick.

Tock.

***

I haven't unpacked because, even though I call this room my own, I know that I'm a fraud. I don't belong here with royalty. I've declined to appear in the news feeds because of publicity issues and my mother, though the king and queen desired to thank me for my service and wanted that to be public. I already told them I haven't served, but they want to thank not only me, but all of Divyeine.

I need to go because the stake that held me down is no longer here. I have no more business here. I have gotten everything I need. I have also lost what I need. I needed Fiomi and Levie, and they left me. Ian has left me, too.

Ian and I are two icebergs, drifting apart across the open sea. I am alone. I want to view Ian with contempt because he seems to have nothing of value to me, but I still care for him. He was and is my best friend, and there is nothing I can do to change that. We are tied to a string. No matter how much we may hate each other, nothing can break us apart.

I slip my backpack on my shoulder and head down the stairs. I find the king and queen settled in the throne room.

"I have to go," I blurt. "I'm sorry."

They blink for a moment, but their faces show understanding. The queen rises and moves toward me, her arms outstretched. Her kind face wrinkles in a somber smile. She gives me a bitter-sweet goodbye. The king smiles at me one last time before I turn on my heel, nod to the guards, and leave the place I now call home.

FIFTY-FIVE

I FIND MYSELF WANDERING TOWARD THE WILLOW. It took me a while to walk here, but with all the thoughts running through my head, it felt like a relatively short walk. This is the place where it all started, so I know I need closure, right here, right now.

I run my hand over the gnarled trunk. The knots and curves sewn into it deliver some sort of closure. A feeling of peace, ancient knowledge, that whatever happened is over. It's done. Also, another kind of closure: accepting that my friends and my love are dead and also saying goodbye to this system. This society is now ruined because it is broken. Things are not in order, and right now no one is able to fix it. I am going to go to the Border, and there is nothing to stop me. But I know I have to save everyone else first.

FIFTY-SIX

THE DIVYEINE GOVERNMENT IS FAR FROM MY HOUSE. My home in Divyeine is surrounded by an expanse of neighborhoods and buildings that serve little use in our system. My home is the farthest from the Willow tree. It's one of the houses right next to the Border. So past my house is just a wall. A very, very tall wall. The grounds are dirt, and the buildings are constructed of concrete block and corrugated iron. Each house has little decoration, at best adorned with a few personal belongings. A flag, maybe, with the Divyeine symbol, a silhouette of a wolf. They said it's to show that wolves are in a pack and that they will be together, but that's a lie. Wolves show dominance, and they sometimes fight. I don't want to know how that turns out. I don't go back to my home. Instead, I go to the government building, which is four enormous concrete slabs pressed together. Two guards stand in the front, holding rifles. I hide on the side of the building, peeking around the corner. One guard is looking the opposite direction of where I am. The guards aren't too big—probably a body mass I can take down. I tiptoe forward a bit. A twig snaps under my foot. Crap. One of the guards perks up and looks around.

"Did you hear a noise?" he asks the other guard.

He looks in my direction. I let out a small gasp.

"Hey!" he says before running toward me. He clenches the rifle tighter while he runs. I had planned to sneak up on one of them and kick their most vulnerable spots, then get the rifle and use the butt of it to smash into the head of the other guard. Now I can't do that.

If I want to stay alive, my only option is to surrender, so I do.

"Hey there, fellas," I say nervously.

The guard stops running a little. "A kid?" he murmurs. "What are you doing here?" he calls out.

"I got lost…" I say, scratching at my nape. I force a smile. "Sorry, I was trying to get to my combat classes, but I wasn't paying attention to where I was going, so I got lost."

The guard seems to buy my act because he lowers his rifle. He's in a close enough vicinity by now. I kick him hard in the shin. He doubles over, groaning. The other guard points his rifle at us but hesitates. I think the guard I kicked is in the way so he can't get a clear shot. To make it worse, I uppercut his face, then kick him in the stomach. The guard falls backward. Dammit, he's more persistent than I thought. He's not letting go of the rifle, even though he's yelling out in pain. I try to use his body to shield myself from the other guard. We struggle with the rifle, and I try to kick him away again in hopes that he'll let go, but he doesn't. Instead, he points the rifle and fires it at my right leg.

Pain shoots through my body, pain worse than what my parents had ever given me. I have never been shot before, and it's not what I expected. It hurts, but more than that, my body just burns, like a fire started spreading from my leg. Crap. I need to stop the bleeding, but I can already feel my body getting weak.

The guard I beat up struggles to stand, but he eventually does, and he and the other guard grab me and shove me through the doors of the building.

Everything seems the same—the iron pillars still bolted to the floor and reaching to the ceiling, the long white desk stretching in a semicircle around the six councilmembers sitting in front of me, hands clasped. They are immersed in conversation, but the conversation ceases when I'm thrown to the ground by the guards. They look at the floor, which is being stained by the blood from my wound. The guard I beat up is still limping, but it is nothing compared to my injury. Then, my eyes land on the faces of the councilmembers, and I almost stumble back and gasp.

One of the councilmembers is familiar. Too familiar. Her long fingernails shine from the light of the lamp hanging over her head. Her graying hair is slicked back in a tightly pulled, impeccable bun. Her eyes are sharp. She sees me and smiles like a cat before catching and eating a small mouse. She curves her back so it is poised in an arch, as if ready to lunge.

My eyes narrow, and I nod to the six Leaders. Then I speak directly to her, giving her my full attention and eye contact. "Hello, Mother," I say.

FIFTY-SEVEN

SMALL MURMURS GO AROUND THE GROUP OF COUNCILMEMBERS. They whisper to each other, their conversations bouncing off the big walls. They glare at me, and I return the dirty look. I recognize Mr. Finne, Leonie's father, sitting at the right end of the table. He really is no better of a father than mine was. His eyes are steely as he looks at me, but underneath, I can see the empathy in his eyes.

"How are you sitting up there, Mother?" I'm somehow still able to talk. Perhaps the shock of being shot and the adrenaline rush makes me a bit stronger.

The councilmembers give me questioning looks.

"The last time I saw you, you were drunk and wasted and you abused me. I assumed the Leaders would still have the honor and decency to not even consider you being a councilmember. But I should've known all of you are stupid."

Mother jerks toward me, but the two councilmembers next to her restrain her.

"You see?" I taunt. "The ones who enforce the law are the ones who commit the crimes. By now, I'm not surprised."

"It doesn't take that long to become sober," Mother says curtly.

The councilmember sitting next to Mother speaks. He has a beard, and his long, thin white hair is combed back neatly. He cocks his head and narrows his eyes. "What happened to you?" he asks.

"Oh, nothing," I say casually, though the edges of my vision are starting to black out. "Just got shot trying to get in here."

"What are you here for?" The councilmember asks.

"The moonstone," I say, eyeing him hard. At this point, I can't see clearly. Three of the councilmembers' eyes go wide. A ripple of conversation spreads through the room. Then, the councilmember with the white beard speaks again.

"We don't need her. Take her away. Also, request for medical attention and get someone to clean this up. I don't want her bleeding all over the floors, and we can't have her dead just yet." He stands, hovering over the table. "Lock her downstairs." The two guards take hold of me. They take me away, but before they do, he speaks one last time.

"Oh, and Micah, we don't have the moonstone. But I think you already know that." Then he laughs, and I am led away to the darkness of the large basement that surrounds me. My vision gets foggy now, and I collapse.

I wake up to a bandaged leg. It's in a splint. How long has it been? The pain has subsided a bit. I probably have some morphine or another pain medicine in my system. The guard I beat up isn't here; he probably went to go get medical attention as well. The other guard sits on a chair away from the wall nearest me, to which I am shackled. I didn't notice what he looked like before—there were too many things going on. He runs a hand through his hair and looks at me. I stagger back as far as I can.

This cannot be happening.

FIFTY-EIGHT

"MICAH." Ian's copper hair is unkempt, swept over his eyes in long tendrils. He looks at me with his muddy green eyes, smiling sadly, though it looks more like a smirk to me. His lips move, whispering words I almost can't comprehend: "You didn't know Divyeine as well as you thought you did."

I understand now. The government building may stand far away from my home, but the councilmembers are all around me. One was even in my home. And I know that what I say to a councilmember doesn't go unnoticed.

"Why are you here?" I say. "How are you here?"

Ian laughs. "I'm finding the moonstone, silly."

"We're supposed to do that together!" I say. The skin around Ian's eyes crinkles as he grins.

"When we last talked, you yelled at me to go here, so I did. But sure, we can do it together." Then, he walks over to me and squats, so his face is level with mine. He takes a silver key from his pocket. The key is cut so it has a design of leaves curling around it. It's tied to a thin, metallic wire: indestrium. Indestrium is a special metal alloy that cannot be cut, so once it's tied or molded to something, there's no taking it off. The metal is called indestrium because it is indestructible. It cannot be broken. He unlocks my cuffs. They fall, skidding across the floor.

"Couldn't you just have shot the other guard when I was outside?" I say irritably. I wouldn't have gotten shot if he had just fired the gun. Then we would've been able to escape together.

"I couldn't. Also, I had to build up rapport for that other guard to trust me a little." He shows me his wrist, where a metal cuff bites into his skin. It looks like indestrium, but I can't be sure.

"What's that for?" I ask, flexing my fingers and rolling my wrists.

"It's an indestrium cuff. It is designed with a bomb mechanism so if I ever go outside of Divyeine, it will detonate. I have to work for them or else I die." So that's why he couldn't shoot the other guard in that moment. Because what would happen if he did? He wouldn't be able to run away, anyway.

A shot of betrayal and anger rushes through me, but I can't

blame him because, really, I did yell at him to come here. "You came here without me, and now you're going to explode. Why would they do that to you?"

Ian smiles at me and wipes at the tears threatening to spill from his eyes. "They know I was the one who met you at the Willow."

Then I remember. Of course. Mother is one of the councilmembers. She's the head of law enforcement, along with the other five. And I'm not supposed to know Ian. Ian and I are traitors.

FIFTY-NINE

"SO HOW WILL WE ESCAPE?" I ask Ian. I examine the shiny cuff on his wrist. He can't be the killer. He wouldn't have come here and gotten himself in this position.

"We don't."

"I know where the moonstone is. I was wrong. It's not here."

Ian looks at me briefly, surprise crossing his face. "What?"

"Yes, the moonstone isn't here. The councilmember who told me the moonstone isn't here has been a councilmember for the longest time. He's the oldest man in Divyeine, and we all know he doesn't lie."

"How can you tell?" Ian says. "Divyeine is the tribe feeding us all the lies. You said so yourself."

"No." I shake my head. "He's one of the good ones. He was kind to me when I was younger. I haven't talked to him in years."

Ian scratches his head. "So why'd he lock you up?"

"Protocol," I spit bitterly.

"Where is the moonstone?" Ian asks.

I turn to him. "It's outside the Border. I know it. No one comes back from there, fighting people we don't even know exist. It only makes sense. They told me Calowell committed suicide. What if he's alive? Ian, we have to go!" Everything is coming together. I know Divyeine could never be truthful, so why did I believe them when they told me what happened to Calowell? It's obvious the moonstone isn't here in Divyeine, so it has to be somewhere else. The labs that Zesten was talking about. They were outside the Border, and maybe Calowell was sent there to supervise? There's one more component I'm missing, but I can't put my finger on it.

Ian shakes his head. "I can't go. This will blow. There's no way I can remove it. A key won't work; they bonded it so I can't take it off. But I'll take you to the edge of Divyeine."

SIXTY

"SO, YOU'RE SURE THIS IS GOING TO WORK?" Ian asks skeptically. The guards had taken my backpack from me, but since Ian was one of them, he was able to retrieve it with my computer in it.

"Yes," I assure him. He sits on the floor of the basement-like room, holding my speedite. A speedite is a computer that has access to everything, including passwords. That's if you use it right. Hackers usually have speedites. Speedite is short for speed of light. The computer works quickly, so experienced hackers who use it can crack codes in seconds, which is especially useful. The light from the speedite casts a shadow on Ian's face. His fingers fly across the keys like a speedite itself. "It will work. It's just that the bomb code is encrypted so securely into the hardware that it's as if there is really nothing there at all."

"Okay," he says slowly, contemplating this thought.

"If it's basically woven into the hardware, all you have to do is unravel it."

SIXTY-ONE

I SAID THAT THE COMPUTER IS A SPEEDITE. It's true. Within five minutes, Ian finally finds the code, and I hear a small click. I grin. "You did it?"

Ian returns the warm look. "I did it."

"How'd you do it?" I ask. The wound on my leg distracts me too much to watch Ian's screen.

Ian smiles at me. "I did what you said. I unraveled it. It was basically a scavenger hunt. I had multiple sets of coding, and I found what was wrong with each code, which was a random letter in the middle. Then, once I'd gathered up those four letters, I tried combinations to see what the code would be." He slides me the speedite. On the brilliantly lit screen, four letters are put in order: D V N E. Wow. The councilmembers of Divyeine are so full of themselves, and not that smart. They certainly didn't get the smart gene. If they were dumb enough to let my mother on the council, their technology is probably not that secure.

"Now we just need to get out. The other guard went upstairs, and I heard the councilmembers saying they were going to their quarters. Is it night already?"

Ian looks at the speedite, his eyes searching for the time. "Yes."

"We need to deal with the other guard."

Ian's positive look falters. "I . . . already dealt with him."

I stare at him. "Ian . . ." I say slowly. "What did you do?"

He scratches the back of his neck. "He probably won't be able to be a guard for a while."

"Did you beat him up or something?" Ian doesn't say anything. Instead, he just gives me a rifle. I take it in my hands and notice the blood spatter on it. He got this gun from the guard.

I purse my lips. That guard must have been severely injured for him not to have his gun on hand. He's probably in a medical facility by now.

Ian tightens his grip on his gun. I walk up the stairs of the basement first, with Ian helping push me up. I'm trying not to put pressure on my leg, but the pain has dulled from the medicine they must have given me.

We emerge from the doorway, and I survey the area. My heart

drops. I should've known. Why would they allow Ian to watch over his best friend? They know we have a connection. Well, they definitely aren't as stupid as I thought because standing at the table I thought would be empty is my mother.

***

"Well," Mother says, checking her stopwatch. "It was about time." She looks at me with a malicious glint in her eye. Her eyes fall to my bandaged leg.

"Ouch. I can't imagine how much that must hurt," she says, with no empathy in her words.

My jaw hardens. "Why are you doing this?" I say through clenched teeth. The memories of her abuse come flooding back. Year after year, I endured the pain she inflicted on me. I was strong-willed and strong-minded. It was a cycle. A new bruise or cut would appear on my body, and I'd simply go to the bathroom, clean it, and put a bandage on it if needed. When we were younger, Ian would always tell me how much he wanted to help me and how he would try to end her abuse, but there was nothing he could've done, and there was nothing I could have done either. I was too young, too naive, and too weak for my own good. I'm not about to let everything I built up crumble down. I have already asked this question before, and she gives me the same answer:

"I'm doing this," she begins, "to help you."

"Bull!" I cry. "Abuse? That was to help me?"

"Well, look how strong you are now. And look at that anger, look at that intent. You're almost starting to look like . . . me."

"I've done things I regret," I say in a shaky voice. "I've said things I regret. But I am nothing like you. What happened to you?" Tears are starting to roll down my face. I can't break now, but my body is betraying me. "What happened to being the mother you were when you read me that poem?"

There's a change in Mother's expression. Surprise crosses her face. "You . . . remember that?"

"Yes, I do. It's the only good memory of you that I have!"

She quickly replaces the surprise with anger. "No," she says. "What happened to you? You used to be so submissive and obedient."

"What happened to me? I grew tired of your bull and decided to end your abuse, that's what! Now answer me, Mother, why couldn't you just be the kind mother who read me that poem?"

"You ruined everything!" she screams. "You ruined my life! I wish I never had you! People had high expectations of me, and I was doing well! How do you think I became a councilmember?

They gave me a break when I had you, but I didn't want that! I had a good life until you were born! You made it so much harder for me. You ruined my dreams, and I couldn't go back until recently, after you left." She sinks down to her knees. This is the first time I have ever seen her weak side.

"So you've finally said it," I say bitterly. "You didn't even try. You just gave up and decided to let all your anger out on me. You reflected the pressure of others' expectations on me. This wasn't to help me. None of it was. This was to help yourself. Turns out you're just a pathetic bitch." I limp to her and clench the rifle in my hands. This would be a good chance to escape, but I have other things on my mind. I point the rifle at her, and she shields her face with her hands.

"Do it," she says. "Pull the trigger." Mother is more exhausted than I have ever seen her. As I stand above her, all I see is a pathetic wreck. Just one swift move and the cause of my pain and suffering will be gone. Just one swift move. My finger shifts on the trigger. One move, and it'll be the end of her. It's so tempting. It's calling out for me, but I just can't do it.

"Micah," Ian says. His voice gives me a wakeup call. I shiver. Was I really about to do that?

I lower the rifle. Mother looks up slowly. "What are you doing?" she asks weakly. "Just kill me already. Get it over with!"

I look down on her. "No," I say coolly. "If I did, I would be just as bad as you, and I won't be stooping to your level." I'm glad Ian called my name before I became unable to keep my overwhelming emotions in check.

Tears stream down Mother's face, but I just look at her in disgust.

"Is there anything I can do to make up for it?" she sobs.

My face darkens. "No," I say. "There is absolutely nothing you can do to make up for what you have done. I will never be able to forgive you, but you can start atoning by giving me a way out. I'm going to the Border gate. I'm sure that you, as a councilmember, would have a key to unlock the gates." I don't know why I'm telling her this. She could easily wake up the other councilmembers and restrain us. But something between us has changed. Maybe it's because of what she admitted. Maybe it's because I realized how pathetic she truly is, trying to uphold a scary and strong demeanor while underneath she's just a selfish, petty woman.

Mother rummages her hand around in her pocket. She then pulls out a keycard and hands it to me. "Here," she says meekly. "This will unlock the Border gates." It's weird seeing her like this. I'm used to her being angry all the time, so it's odd to see her look so weak in front of me. As much as it repulses me, I feel a pang of pity for her. Why should I feel bad for the woman who ruined my childhood? Just goes to show how different I am from my mother.

Mother falls back onto one of the chairs at the table. I turn to the exit and begin walking toward it with Ian's help. The pain medicine allows me to put some pressure on my leg, so I can walk, just not very well.

I stop walking for a moment. "Goodbye, Mother," I say without looking behind me. Then I continue walking.

Ian packs the speedite in my backpack and holds his hand out to me. I take it. We're really going. The doors open in front of us, and Ian and I slip out into the dark night.

SIXTY-TWO

IAN AND I RUN FOR A LONG TIME, with Ian carrying me most of the way and helping me walk the rest. We run past the familiar houses, past the training grounds, past the poorly built school. I don't look back. I just keep running. I don't know where we are headed, yet I keep going. We need to find the Border. My legs ache, and my chest burns. Ian and I are still holding hands. Eventually, we reach a metal gate I've never seen before. I've walked past it, sure, but I never really wondered what was here, behind the Divyeine soldiers who stood guard. Since there is so much chaos going on, those soldiers must have left their posts to deal with other problems.

This metal gate is thick, most likely made with indestrium. The air has changed. It's colder, more unwelcoming.

"This is it," I breathe. There's a wood board with spray painted words hung on the indestrium. KEEP OUT, it shouts. It doesn't look intimidating. It looks more enticing than threatening, like it's beckoning us in instead of keeping us away. I slide the keycard in the slot, and the gate clicks. I try pushing open the gate, and it opens. I expect a whole other world beyond the gates. This is the only exit from Auneaire, and I'm finally going through it. Finally. But as I open the gates, my jaw drops. I shudder as I see it across the vast expanse of land: ash. I didn't expect fresh air to smell bitter, but it does, and I choke on it. I can see the source of the putrid smell on the horizon.

I expected a whole other world. There was, but now it's burned. It was a village. And in front of the village are the labs. Or what is left of the labs. The village was so close to us. It could probably take me an hour and a half run to get there from the Border. Not far at all. Ian and I walk fast, trying to get to what look like extremely damaged laboratories to see if we can find the moonstone, but there's nothing but ash and debris. It only takes us about forty-five minutes, which means that the village and the labs were closer to Auneaire than I anticipated. Bodies litter the ground. Humans. Like us. They were exactly like us, and they were killed. All this destruction must have taken place years ago. I was too young to know if anything odd was going on, and the village is seemingly far enough from the Border to avoid arousing suspicion from anyone else. How long ago did this happen? If these are the labs, then how long has the moonstone been missing? And how long have Kieling and Divyeine kept their feud under wraps? Their fight over the moonstone must have been going on for so long that the person who created the prophecy got impatient. The moonstone is precious, so no wonder someone would be impatient.

Blood stains the ground, and under my breath I mumble a small apology to the Earth beneath my feet, but I know She doesn't hear. I just pretend She does. My eyes stop on a flash of light reflecting off a badge. That's when I run.

The body is just a pile of dust and dirty bones. Just his bones. No skull. But the fabric is still here, stitched with bold black letters: Chris Calowell. He was here. He fought here. No, he didn't battle. It seems as though they just burned everything to the ground. Anyone who worked here was helpless. But just because they're helpless doesn't mean they're innocent.

SIXTY-THREE

"HE WAS HERE," I CHOKE AND KNEEL NEXT TO HIM. I find it hard to breathe as I finger my mentor's silver badge. The silver is tarnished, but I can still see his name on it. Like how his uniform has been covered in layers of debris and dust for years, yet his name stitched onto it is still visible.

I check his pockets for anything useful, and my fingers grasp a small, brittle piece of paper. My eyes follow the words, hungry for something about me, but I realize that the whole letter is addressed to me. It reads:

Dear Micah,

So much has happened. I cannot think about how much pain you must be in. I'm so sorry I left you, but I didn't have a choice. I am writing something extremely important, so you need to pay attention. Be careful, Micah. The people you think you can trust will deceive you. Divyeine isn't what it was. You need to get out of there. I know there are things going on with your family, which is even more reason to get out. Remember that boy you told me about? Well, find him. Because his life is in danger, and so are the lives of all the others. You're so young, Micah, so I'm sorry you have to read this now. They lied to you. Kieling took a moonstone they shouldn't have taken. Kieling studied it here and promised to study it for only four years. And for four years, the labs did study the moonstone. But they found out what the moonstone is worth, the power it holds. They didn't give it back on the promised date. They lost it. So Divyeine sent soldiers back to the city, back to this place, the place where I'm writing this now. Divyeine ordered us to kill everyone in the labs, and we had no choice but to obey. I didn't, of course, and now my time is up. In one hour I will be executed for treason because I didn't follow Divyeine. I know you know about the Border. No one came back because Divyeine didn't want the rest of Auneaire to know the power the moonstone holds. So everyone here who studied the moonstone was murdered, and the soldiers who murdered the scientists were executed because no one can know. And it goes on. Be careful, Micah. Divyeine is more dangerous than you can ever imagine. Thank you for showing me the light. I'm glad I got to know you.

    Love,

    Chris Calowell,

    Your friend

A tear rolls down my face. I wipe it away. "We should check to see if he has anything else."

Ian doesn't respond, but he crouches and picks up Chris's hat, which he turns over to inspect the inside of. I finger Chris's boots. They must be the same ones he wore when we trained together. When we hung out, he told me he always kept a second gun, or knife, or some sort of weapon in them. I turn them upside down and shake.

But what falls out isn't a weapon. It's a stone. And not just any stone—the moonstone.

"It's here," I say, shaking my head. "It was in his boot, and they killed him without knowing it. They just left him here." I almost laugh at how absurd the whole situation is. "Now that we have the moonstone, we can head back to the Divyeine government building and give it back to them. I don't like the thought of us doing their dirty work, but at least the world will be saved."

"They seemed so collected when they told us they didn't have the moonstone." Ian shivers. "It was weird. I'm sure they'll be glad to have it back."

This is it. All we need to do now is go back to Divyeine, and we can save our whole society. I hook my arm over Ian's neck for support, and we start walking back.

Most of the rest of the way, he carries me while I hold onto the moonstone for safekeeping. I don't feel comfortable putting it in my bag for fear of it falling out. I study the stone. It's about the size of my palm, and while it's quite opalescent, it has a nice glittery hue. It's very pretty and precious. I clasp my hands over it tighter.

Ian starts to slow down, so I look up. It's not where I thought we would stop. We're at the Willow.

"What are we doing here?" I haven't been here alone with Ian since that night. It feels weird to be here. The sun is beginning to set. That much time has passed already?

"Let's take a little break," Ian says.

"Honestly," I say, "sounds good to me. I need to change my bandages anyway." I luckily have some bandages in my bag. I settle down with my back facing Ian. I put the moonstone in my bag and take out the bandages. The pain reliever still hasn't worn off, which is good. I begin to unravel my old bandages.

Behind me, the grass rustles from Ian's footsteps. I don't pay any attention to it. Then, from behind me, Ian presses the tip of a knife to my side.

"Things need to stay the way they are," Ian says.

I struggle to say something, but he just shushes me. My heart falls. I knew it. It was him. It is him. He's the killer.

"I need to confess something," Ian admits to me. I know what he's going to say, and I don't want to hear it. But if I want to listen or not, I know I have to. I feel the knife press deeper into my side, the jagged blade breaking a thin layer of my skin underneath my shirt.

"Yes?" I ask, fear making sweat pool around my brow. He's saying this now because I cannot control anything.

"My parents kicked me out because I wasn't accepted into Larveson's top music school." That's harsh, but what does that have to do with anything?

Tears well in my eyes, and my vision goes blurry.

"Apart from that, that's not what I wanted to confess. I was the one who created the prophecy."

"How?" I croak. "And why?"

"It's not hard to put something in a newspaper. And as for why, it was because of Levie. You love Levie and not me. Do you know how angry that makes someone?"

I do now. But something doesn't add up. I'm afraid to talk, but I know I have to. "But the prophecy was in the newspaper before I even met Levie."

"You love Levie," Ian repeats. He doesn't answer my question, so when he speaks again, I try to focus on him instead of going back to the thought that Ian was the one behind this.

"Three of us were to die. I knew you had to be part of it. So, even though it doesn't mention any names, it was you. And it was that trio. Fate was set, and no matter how much anyone tried to stop it, it could not be stopped. Because remember, I wrote a prophecy. I happen to be good with words. I am, after all, a song-writer. You tried to protect Levie. Your love. It's almost funny, the irony. How the one you wish was dead is alive, and the one you wish was alive is dead. The one you love is dead. You know, you left me in the dark. You left me for him."

I can't jump to conclusions yet. There's no denying that he is in a position to kill me. I have been training all my life for situations like this, but I stay put. Something about this just isn't right.

"I was so happy to see you. But was that it? You just found me? You went to that party to kill me? Three of us were to die, Ian. Not four."

I laugh cruelly because I know I have no chance of living now. "If you're such a good songwriter, why weren't you accepted into that school? Why did you write three instead of four? It's not meant to be." But it is. It's meant to be. I'm not getting out of this. A wash of negative emotions are rushing out from both our lips.

I need to look at him. I can't accept it. What I feel doesn't match the desperate words coming out of my mouth. Then, a sudden sharp pain spreads through me. Ian pulls out the knife, dripping with blood, from my torso. I stumble back. The pain is worse than the gunshot wound was. I fall back and stare into Ian's eyes as he hovers over me.

He looks at me, but when he does, there is no anger in his eyes anymore. There is no more of that burning jealousy I saw a second ago. "I'm doing this to save you!" he says. "Don't you understand? I promised you I would save you, and I'm doing it here, right now." Those are the only words coming out of his mouth that I clearly understand. *I'm doing it to save you.*

And like that, all my built-up anger, all my hurtful words, everything just breaks. Because I understand everything. I understand his intent, his motives, and for the first time in a long time, what's running through his head.

SIXTY-FOUR

"HI," HE HAD SAID. "I haven't seen you here before."

I didn't know what to say. This was my first time ever talking to someone outside of my tribe. It didn't feel as different as I thought it would.

I fidgeted and started scratching my hand. I was nervous, but I soon grew out of that nervousness. The boy looked behind me.

"Hey..." he said slowly, shining his lantern on my face. "You came from Divyeine...didn't you?"

Again, I didn't know what to say to that. I just stared at him. Would he hate me? Would he turn me over to the officials? No, he didn't seem that way. There seemed to be a buzzing energy around him as he looked at me with those big, hazel eyes.

"You don't look like a rule breaker, yet here you are," he noted, eyeing me. "Guess it got a little boring in there, huh? It doesn't seem like you're the type of girl who'd have a lot of friends either."

That was true. I really had no one, not even my own parents to be close to. No one to share the good experiences with, and no one to lean on when I shared the bad. I nodded.

"I don't have any friends," I had said, so quietly that it seemed like he didn't hear me.

The shadow cast by the lantern made part of his face dark and hard to see. I felt a little scared, but then he smiled.

A boy from another tribe smiled at me. His tan skin crinkled as his smile grew wider. He set down the lantern and held out his hand. "Hi," he said, once again. "I'm Ian. I'm gonna be your first friend."

***

"Promise me," I say, grasping Ian's calloused hands in mine. "Promise me that when this is all over, we can start over."

He is silent for a moment. "Okay," he says. "I promise."

Then, we lie on the grass, staring up at the moon under the Willow where it all started. I wanted the end of the old era to create new memories and be the beginning of a new friendship. Fate was always a big thing for us, as I said. It's how we met; it's how we reunited. So in our next life, in that new beginning, fate would bring us together again. The strands of our promise wouldn't break, not like they did the last time.

I squeeze Ian's hand tighter to make sure he will never let go, and as we stare at the stars, I know he won't. He can't. His hand is already cold from the touch of death, and I smile at the stars as life bleeds out of me. But it is a lie. Things are never as they seem. Because he promised he would save me, but save me from what? Living. He would save me from living because that is the only way he knows to save me from this wretched world. It is the only way we could ever meet in the next life because what if the only next life we'll ever be in is the dark abyss of death?

I understand his jealousy, and I understand where he's coming from. I should be angry, like I initially was. I should be scared, but I'm not. All I feel is love, dying right here, next to my best friend, the first person who ever gave me comfort and the first person who ever gave me love, regardless of whether it was platonic or romantic.

This was never about the prophecy, or Auneaire, because why would we go to such lengths to save a world that didn't do us any good in the first place? All this circled back to us, here, dying next to each other under the Willow, which is the symbol of life. We're back where we started. I'm dying under the tree where my life really began.

I made a mistake. I was wrong about Ian. I thought I was done with him. I felt so angry and so frustrated with my feelings that I didn't think our friendship would suffice anymore, but it does. We're here, right now. I'm dying with my first love. I miss Levie, I do, but time has passed and my feelings have once again changed because I believe that all I wanted from Levie was the love I thought Ian couldn't give anymore. I love Ian, and I love him too much. We did so much for each other. Ian loves me so much he's willing to sacrifice himself to die with me. For some reason, I accept death. It's so wrong, but it feels so right. My body is weak. I twitch my fingers, but it's hard to. I continue staring at the stars.

I love Ian. That's the fact that both Ian and I wouldn't accept. I accept it now. I embrace that fact with open arms. Why did I push that fact away? Was it because I was trying to convince myself that love at seven years old wasn't real? That I would grow out of it? That it was merely a feeling that would eventually pass? We finally accepted the strength of our love, but it's also our downfall. At a point, we were both ripped apart by the toxicity of love. Love is poison. Our love is poison. It's how both of us are dying now.

We love each other too much, to the point where we became

twisted with the idea of it. It corrupted us. Perhaps it's better if the next life is nothing, or if we don't find each other again. Then, if there really is a next life, once we reach the end of it, our endings may not be as tragic. No, I love him too much for that to happen. I want to meet again in the next life. I'm done pushing the best things away.

I smile one last time. "Ian," I say. There's no answer, just like that night. But this time, I accept his silence because it allows me to say the words I was too cowardly to say when he was listening.

"Ian." I call out his name one more time. "I love you, and I'm sorry." There's a knot in my stomach and a lump in my throat. I allow tears to roll down my cheeks. I don't hold it in. The stars twinkle. The moon brightly glows. It smiles at me like it did that night. In the moonlight, the green tendrils of the Willow gleam. Warmth spreads through my body as it is slowly enveloped in the spreading of my blood. I never stop holding Ian's calloused hand. I stare at the stars one last time, all the while smiling through my tears. And with my last dying breath, I succumb to Death, who holds out his hand, my body stilling into eternal dormancy, my reverie of thoughts receding into silence.

EPILOGUE

A BOY STANDS AT THE EDGE OF AN OVERHANG, close enough so he can see the roaring current of water falling in front of him and crashing on the flat rocks below, but far enough back that he's not susceptible to any permanent injuries. He turns around to face the girl behind him. Her hair is a flaming red. Her skin looks ghostly pale in the gray light the couple is illuminated with. She's wearing a white dress and ballet shoes, exactly the opposite of what she should be wearing when someone has died. As for the boy, he wears something to match: a white button-down, gray flannel dress pants, and black leather oxfords. She extends her hand, waiting for a quick kiss to be planted on her fingers. The boy doesn't hesitate to lean down to swiftly brush his lips against the girl's fingertips, and the girl withdraws her hand, satisfied.

"She's dead?" the girl smirks, eyebrows arched.

"She's dead," the boy answers, running a hand through his golden hair. His blue eyes are clearer than the murky water below, his mind too. "I've never felt this free." Since Natalia's death in the cabin, Micah's death under the Willow, and Ian's suicide just a few feet away from Micah's body, the waterfall the five leaders had once deemed a safe haven now was considered as a death site and a hideout for those who needed to be tucked away in the little secret cave high above the pool, the waterfall obscuring the hideout from the rest of Auneaire. Though the water was once looked at as clean, the harrowing memories of Natalia's gruesome death in the cabin made the water seem muddy and threatening.

The girl moves closer to the boy. "So you don't feel guilty?" Their faces are close. Too close.

"No," he says, drawing his lips to hers. Almost. She toys with him, moving before he can kiss her. She smirks.

"I almost feel sorry for her. For him. They really believed I was dead. Of course, they should have known that they didn't find a body, only my burned flesh. People jump to conclusions so quickly." She tilts her head in such a manner that she really does seem sorry. She paints her face with a little pout to hide the discomfort that continues to flare through her because of the raw, seared flesh on her leg, covered only by a thin layer of bandages.

The boy responds to the girl, who is now standing next to him, staring at the water running down in front of them. "You shouldn't be sorry. They were being ignorant. She didn't think that she out of the five leaders could be one of the dead. As for Ian, he was just crazy."

"He wasn't even a part of this," she says.

"It was easy to manipulate them. You would've enjoyed doing that," the boy says.

"They should be easy to manipulate. I mean, getting into Ian's head about her loving you? I'm glad it worked!"

"Well, part of that was just luck. If it weren't for Ian's dysphagia caused by a head injury and the unsaid fact that maybe the injury was worse than they thought, we might've never succeeded in manipulating him."

"I give you all the credit for that," the girl says, leaning on the boy. "Using his head injury to brainwash him into a complicated story that he was never behind? Genius! He's really just crazy after all. Something happened, and I don't think it was our doing. He said that he was saving her. She didn't even fight after he said that. The way he said it, it made it seem like it was something they had talked about before."

The boy snorts and crosses his arms. "Yeah, it probably was, but who cares? Both of them are now out of the way. I don't feel bad for manipulating her. It looked like she really thought I loved her. And when I had my supposed death, it was extremely easy to leave. Everyone was freaking out about the body. They're never going to find the body is fake. You can't discover a fake body when you don't even exist anymore." He pauses, then continues.

"All of it was just a ruse. She's dead, and I never loved her. But in the end, I have what I want, so it doesn't matter anymore. Speaking of what I want, do you have it?" the boy asks.

"I do." The girl simpers, drawing a sparkling stone out of her pocketbook. She hands it to the boy. He takes it from her and snickers.

"We did it. Congrats." The boy grins. "But this was all you."

"Are you kidding? We did this together. We worked on this together. And it all started with putting a prophecy in the Divyeine newspaper. I suppose they aren't as smart as they think they are," the girl says.

"You're right. We did this. We started this, Fiomi." He lets the name roll off his tongue.

"And now we're going to end it. All of it." Fiomi laughs humorlessly.

"Are you ready?" he asks.

"I've always been ready, Levian." She pulls him closer, gripping the front of his button-down, finally giving him the kiss he had wanted since the start.

ACKNOWLEDGMENTS

I began writing Auneaire in 2019 while my twin brother rehearsed for his debut solo with the Stanford Symphonic Chorus. Two years later, self-publishing my first book was much harder than I ever imagined. Feedback from family and friends, countless revisions, and professional editing shaped Auneaire into the final product it is today—naturally imperfect, but incrementally better with each pass.

I express my gratitude to my mom and dad for supporting me throughout my writing adventure. From early drafts onward, reading and editing my manuscript inspired me to seek amazing professional editors, a book designer, and cover artist. Thank you for taking time to reflect on my ideas and suggesting ways to improve my work. You both did so much.

I thank Melissa Aranzamendez—my godmother—the first person to read and edit my early draft. I relish your kind words of encouragement and sharing helpful sites to find book editors. Were it not for you, I'd never know my wonderful editors Sean and Sarah.

Special thanks go to my developmental editor Sean Fletcher, my copy editor Sarah Barker, and my proofreader Kayla Ramoutar. You did such a thorough job scrubbing my manuscript. With your professional touch, I completed the editorial process with you all at my side.

Heartfelt thanks go to my book designer, Veronica Scott, who formatted each page and chapter to flow seamlessly—front-to-back—and to my cover illustrator, Carlo Tano, who magically morphed my ideas into mesmerizing imagery of the lead characters. I always held that a book's appearance is as important to stimulate the reader's imagination and excitement as are words themselves. You both captured the key design aspects that I had always imagined. Thank you for your talents.

I thank Stephanie Sassoon—a close family friend—who volunteered innumerable hours reading and editing one of the earliest versions of my manuscript, and to my English teacher, Mrs. Stephanie Vance, for reading my book and providing invaluable feedback. Your help, support, and encouragement powered me through to completion.

Big thanks go to my siblings Andrea, Austen, and Liam, and all my relatives and extended family who supported me throughout this arduous trek.

Thank you also to my close friends Gia, Cailey, Yana, and Raquel. You gave me space to rant passionately about the backstories and emotions of my characters—even before you read the first chapter. Thank you for being so encouraging when I was sharing my early ideas. I am grateful for your love and support.

And finally, thank you to all others who supported and believed in me on this incredible journey—if even in the smallest ways.

I hope you enjoy reading Auneaire as much as I enjoyed writing it.

Mira Lowitz

Made in the USA
Middletown, DE
10 December 2021

54966284R10146